Welcome to W🕶NDERLAND

BEACH BATTLE
BLOWOUT

Favorites by
CHRIS GRABENSTEIN

The Island of Dr. Libris
Shine! (coauthored with J.J. Grabenstein)

THE MR. LEMONCELLO'S LIBRARY SERIES
Escape from Mr. Lemoncello's Library
Mr. Lemoncello's Library Olympics
Mr. Lemoncello's Great Library Race
Mr. Lemoncello's All-Star Breakout Game
Mr. Lemoncello and the Titanium Ticket

THE WELCOME TO WONDERLAND SERIES
Home Sweet Motel
Beach Party Surf Monkey
Sandapalooza Shake-Up
Beach Battle Blowout

THE HAUNTED MYSTERY SERIES
The Crossroads
The Demons' Door
The Zombie Awakening
The Black Heart Crypt

COAUTHORED WITH JAMES PATTERSON
The House of Robots series
The I Funny series
The Jacky Ha-Ha series
Katt vs. Dogg
The Max Einstein series
Pottymouth and Stoopid
The Treasure Hunters series
Word of Mouse

BEACH BATTLE BLOWOUT

• Book 4 •

CHRIS GRABENSTEIN

illustrated by Kelly Kennedy

A Yearling Book

Text copyright © 2019 by Chris Grabenstein
Cover art copyright © 2019 by Brooklyn Allen
Interior illustrations copyright © 2019 by Kelly Kennedy

Visit us on the Web! rhcbooks.com

Educators and librarians, for a variety of teaching tools, visit us at RHTeachersLibrarians.com

The Library of Congress has cataloged the hardcover edition of this work as follows:
Names: Grabenstein, Chris, author.
Title: Beach battle blowout / by Chris Grabenstein.
Description: First edition. | New York : Random House, [2019] |
Series: Welcome to Wonderland ; #4 | Summary: P.T. and Gloria
need a great plan to ensure the Wonderland can beat a slick
new attraction in the "Fun in the Sun" contest.
Identifiers: LCCN 2017006197 | ISBN 978-1-5247-1762-9 (hardcover) |
ISBN 978-1-5247-1764-3 (ebook)
Subjects: | CYAC: Hotels, motels, etc.—Fiction. | Contests—Fiction. |
Friendship—Fiction.
Classification: LCC PZ7.G7487 Bb 2019 | DDC [Fic]—dc23

ISBN 978-1-5247-1763-6 (paperback)

Printed in the United States of America
10 9 8 7 6 5 4 3 2 1
First Yearling Edition 2020

For the late Thomas Aloysius Grabenstein—
my dad

BEACH BATTLE
BLOWOUT

Duel with the Dolphin King

"This weekend," I told my audience, "I had a duel with a dolphin."

"Whaaaa?" said everybody else.

Fact: when you live in a motel, you always have the best stories on Monday mornings.

"The Wonderland's right on the beach," I told my history class. "So I grew up speaking Dolphin."

I gave a quick demo. "*Eeeek squeeeee, klik-klik.*"

"What's that mean?" asked my bud Bruce Brandow.

"'I have to go to the bathroom.'"

"Dolphins say that?"

"Yep. Then they do it. Right there in the Gulf. That's why the water's so warm."

"Gross," said Bruce.

We were between bells, just waiting for our

teacher, Mr. Frumpkes, to march in and put us all to sleep with a barrage of boring facts. It was up to me to spin a story so scintillating it could fight off the Frumpkes Funk.

"On Saturday, I was riding the waves, just surfing along—"

"Surfing?" scoffed Adam Shapera, a big guy who always sits in the back of the room so it's easier to flick people's ears. "Who taught you how to do that?"

"Kevin the Monkey," said my good friend Gloria Ortega. "Star of the smash hit *Beach Party Surf Monkey.*"

Unimpressed, Adam blew a lip fart.

I didn't let Adam slow me down, because everybody else was hanging on my every word, scooching their seats closer.

"I was carving across a wave. Totally cranking. It was epic. All of a sudden, out of nowhere, this dolphin pops up!"

"The dolphin blew his airhole at me. It sounded like one of Adam Shapera's lip farts. It spooked me so much I wiped out."

"What'd the dolphin want?" asked Bruce.

"To challenge me to a friendly competition." I put on my best high-pitched dolphin voice. "'I am Frederick, the Dolphin King. I challenge you to a duel!'"

"Whoa," said Bruce. "Just like that Alexander Hamilton dude with that other dude."

"Aaron Burr," said Gloria.

"Exactly," I said. "But we wouldn't be dueling with pistols. It'd be unfair. Dolphins don't have trigger fingers."

"That's so true," said Adam, finally getting into the story with everybody else.

"We decided on a race," I said. "From the Gulf waters behind the Wonderland all the way up St. Pete Beach to the Don CeSar Hotel. It'd be me and my board against King Frederick and his mighty flippers. Human against dolphin. Mano a mammalo. I, of course, agreed to King Frederick's terms. But only because I knew I'd win."

"How'd you know that?" Adam asked eagerly.

"Simple," I told him. "I was carrying a secret weapon!"

King of the Seas

"**S**ix other dolphins surrounded King Fred," I said, then switched back to my squeaky dolphin voice. "'Make a lane, oh loyal subjects! Three of thee on either side.'"

Gloria had her fingers jammed in her ears. She hates when I do Dolphin. She says it sounds like a fork scraping across her teeth.

"The dolphins split up, formed two lines. The king and I were in the middle—me on my board, him on his belly. The Dolphin King squealed, *'Kaaah! Quee! Eeek!'* and the race was on! He shot off to an early lead. But remember—I still had my secret weapon!"

"So, what was it?" asked Bruce, who couldn't stand the suspense, which, by the way, is a very important part of any story. Because if the thread

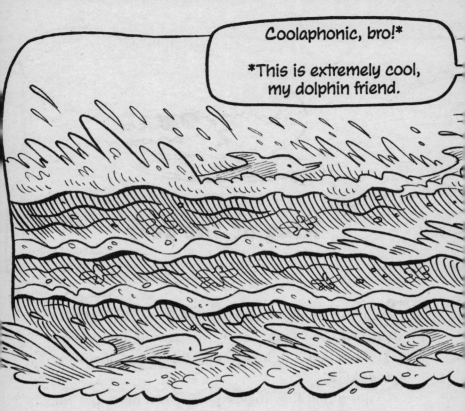

of your story leaves your audience dangling, they won't dare let go.

"You ever heard of kitesurfing?" I asked him.

"Sure."

"Well, Fred the Dolphin King hadn't. Imagine his surprise when I unfurled my kite, caught a tailwind, and flew up the Gulf at forty-six miles per hour."

"That's forty knots," explained Gloria, after she tapped her calculator. My best friend is a business

squee-chee-klik-
klik, skronk!*

*Cowabunga,
dude.

wiz. Her calculator is always fired up and ready to
crunch numbers.

"Since the rules of our race didn't specifically
prohibit kites or outboard motors or *anything*, the
Dolphin King graciously admitted defeat when he
and his pals finally caught up with me at the finish
line. He offered me his crown, but I told him, 'No
thanks, King Fred. Winning is its own reward.'"

"Cool," said Bruce.

"Yeah. I read that in a fortune cookie once."

In the back row, Adam was raising his hand. He had an extremely skeptical look on his face.

"Yes?" I said.

"Where'd you stash all your secret gear? The kite, the harness, and the towlines?"

"In my board shorts, bro."

The whole class, including Adam, cracked up.

Yep, everybody in the classroom was laughing.

Except our teacher, Mr. Frumpkes.

He was standing in the doorway, scowling at me.

Grumpy Mr. Frumpkes

"Do you know what we call this class, Mr. Wilkie?" asked Mr. Frumpkes, both hands jabbed against his bony hips so he could glare at me even harder.

"History, sir," I replied. "Unless, of course, you want to switch it to recess, which would be awesome. Adam Shapera brought his soccer ball."

Mr. Frumpkes blinked repeatedly. His glasses magnified his flickering eyelashes so much they looked like moths dancing near a bonfire.

"Mr. Wilkie," Mr. Frumpkes fumed, "this is, indeed, history. A class where we study facts. We do not regale our classmates with implausible recitations of untruths such as your ridiculous tale about the Dolphin King. Dolphins do not communicate with humans, and they do not have kings."

"Are you sure, sir?" asked Adam from the back

Recess is not a class, Mr. Wilkie! It is a hollowed-out space, much like your skull, which is clearly empty, since you don't have a brain!

row. "My little sister has a hair clip shaped like a dolphin, and it's wearing a sparkly gold crown."

"I saw a talking dolphin in a TV commercial," said Bruce. "I think it was for swimming pool supplies. . . ."

Mr. Frumpkes closed his eyes. "Do you see what you have done, Phineas Taylor Wilkie?"

Fact: whenever Mr. Frumpkes is really seriously

annoyed with me, he calls me by my full name instead of just P.T.

"You have warped your classmates' impressionable young minds with your preposterous whoppers."

Gloria raised her hand.

"Now what?" said Mr. Frumpkes, clearly seething. "Do you have a problem, Miss Ortega?"

"No problem here, sir," said Gloria. "However, if you are referring to Whoppers, the malted milk balls manufactured by the Hershey Company, *you* may have a problem. Whoppers is a registered trademark and, as such, can't be used without written consent from the Hershey legal department."

"Never mind!" hollered Mr. Frumpkes, his face going code purple. "Open your books. Today we will be learning about another famous Floridian— the Miami pharmacist who, in 1944, developed the first widely used sunscreen. . . ."

And blah-blah-blah for almost an hour. When the bell finally rang, Mr. Frumpkes was telling us how Ponce de León had planted Florida's first orange trees "sometime between 1513 and 1565."

A fifty-two-year period.

Which is exactly how long a period in Mr. Frumpkes's history class usually feels.

After-School Activities

Gloria and I always ride the bus home together after school when she doesn't have a Junior Achievement meeting with her fellow business-loving buds.

Gloria and her dad are "extended stay" guests at my family's wacky motel on St. Pete Beach because her father is a sportscaster for WTSP, channel ten. When you work in TV, you change jobs a lot. Cities, too. Gloria and Mr. Ortega have lived in Scranton, Buffalo, Chattanooga, and Tucson (to name just a few), where he worked for WNEP, WKBW, WRCB, and KVOA, respectively.

Fact: when you work in broadcasting, your life becomes a gigantic jumble of letters with lots of extra Ws. It's kind of like playing Boggle.

Since the Ortegas don't know how long they'll be living in Florida before they move on to their next

TV gig, staying at a motel makes more sense than buying a house.

It's also more fun, especially for Gloria. If you're a kid, our motel is the best place on earth to call home.

Think about it: There's a swimming pool, a miniature golf course, goofy decorations, a beach, a video game room, and all the ice cubes you could ever need. Someone vacuums your room and makes your bed every day and (here's the best part) it isn't you! There's a hair dryer in the bathroom and a microwave in the bedroom, so your zapping needs are totally covered. Did I mention the free Wi-Fi and cable TV, plus vending machines filled with convenient snack-food items and frosty beverages, plus, out back, the Banana Shack, where hamburgers sizzle on an open grill night and day?

Fact: the Wonderland Motel is kid heaven.

The school bus chugged down Gulf Boulevard, dropping people off every three or four blocks.

"Hey, there's the WTSP news van," said Gloria as we neared the bus stop one away from our own.

The TV station's truck, with a satellite dish and a forest of antennas on top, was parked in front of a brand-new boxy building that looked like a flamingo-pink and neon-green castle. Its freshly paved parking lot was decorated with Grand Opening! banners and balloons. A flashy sign out front labeled it the Fun Castle. A video screen promised Climbing Walls! Skee-Ball! Trampolines! Ball Crawls! And the Most Amazing Indoor Golf Course Ever—the Mega Mini!

"Wow," said Gloria as we both gawked at the sign, with all its magical promises. "I wonder if Dad's in there reporting for WTSP."

"Let's go find out," I suggested.

We grabbed our backpacks and headed up the aisle.

"This isn't your stop, kids," said the driver, a nice lady named Ms. Terbock, who *loves* our Wonderland shampoo because it smells like coconuts mixed with limes. (I give Ms. Terbock a ton of the tiny bottles on special holidays I make up during the school year, such as National Drive a Bunch of Kids to School Day.)

"We want to see if my dad's inside," said Gloria.

Ms. Terbock swung open the door for the kids who usually hopped off at that stop.

"Ooh, your father is soooo handsome," she said, practically swooning. "You know, I never enjoyed sports until your father came to town. I still don't. But I *love* him!"

Gloria laughed.

"See you tomorrow, Ms. Terbock," I said. "It's National Hair Conditioner Day!"

"Sweet!"

Gloria and I bounded down the stairs. The letters on the Fun Castle's video screen flipped and spun into a sparkling message: Welcome to St. Pete Beach's New Home for Fun in the Sun.

Huh.

I figured that meant the Wonderland was its *old* home.

The Fun Bunch

"Hey, ho, kiddos!" said a high-school-aged guy in khaki shorts and a polo shirt.

He and a girl were passing out slick brochures in the Fun Castle parking lot.

"If you're looking for fun in the sun, you're in the right spot!" said the girl. "Sir Laughsalot welcomes you to the grand opening of his all-new, all-awesome, all-fun Fun Castle!"

The two cheery greeters had smiles brighter than Mr. Ortega's, and his is a three-hundred-watter. Behind them, a goofy guy in an Alligator King costume was doing herky-jerky dance moves like a baseball team mascot. I figured he was Sir Laughsalot. I wondered if he knew the Dolphin King.

"Um, do you know who's here from WTSP?" asked Gloria.

"The one and only super-fun Manny Ortega!" said the chipper girl. "We swapped whitening-strip tips."

Gloria rolled her eyes. "Of course you did."

"We're from the Wonderland Motel," I said. "Three blocks down Gulf Boulevard."

"The Wonderland?" said the guy, shaking his head and frowning. "Ouch. That's the motel where the staff steals stuff, right?"

"Wrong. They were framed. *We* were framed."

I was going to give him a blow-by-blow of

everything that had happened during what I like to call the Sandapalooza Shake-Up, but I could tell the guy wasn't paying attention.

So I changed the subject. "How much does it cost to go in and take a look around?"

"Nada," said the girl, her smile widening. "That's Spanish for 'nothing'!"

"We know," said Gloria. *"Mi abuelo es de Cuba."*

The girl stared blankly at Gloria for a few seconds. Then she said, "Awesome!"

"Have fun, kiddos!" said the guy.

"Because at the Fun Castle," said the girl, "fun is job one!"

"You're supposed to say, 'Fun *in the sun* is job one,'" whispered her partner.

"But the building has a roof," the girl whispered back. "There isn't any sun inside."

"So?" said the guy through clenched teeth. "It's in the manual. Stay on script, Heather, or Bradley will fire you so fast—"

"Don't worry about me, Todd. Worry about you."

"What?"

"Your polo shirt is untucked! Bradley hates an untucked polo. . . ."

They both seemed super tense.

While Todd hurriedly tucked in his shirt, Gloria and I slipped away. But I couldn't stop thinking about what Todd had just said.

Recently my family's motel had (barely) survived what business wizards like Gloria call a "public relations disaster." Nobody on our staff had done anything wrong, but some people were saying they had—loudly—so others figured it had to be true.

Once our housekeepers and cook were cleared, we began slowly crawling back into the black. That meant we were almost making money again.

But I knew the truth: the Wonderland needed another major boost. Some kind of gimmick or publicity stunt big enough to make everybody forget every bad thing they'd ever heard on the radio or read about us online.

If we didn't get that soon, our days of fun in the sun would be done.

Funshine

"**H**ey, ho, kiddos!" chirped another cheery guy in a polo shirt and khaki shorts when we entered the Fun Castle.

His name tag ID'd him as Bradley. His shirt was tucked in. Tight.

I figured he was the boss, the one Todd and Heather were so afraid of. Bradley was in his twenties and extremely buff. It looked like he bench-pressed benches. The kind made out of concrete.

The Fun Castle was dark and noisy. Bells dinged. Kids whooted. Wooden balls clacked. Video games warbled. Thumping music pumped out of ceiling speakers.

"Welcome to the all-new, all-fun Fun Castle!" our inside greeter shouted. "I'm Bradley, the master funmeister here. It's my job to make sure you kid-dos have the most fun under the sun."

"But there's a roof," said Gloria, pointing toward the ceiling. "There's no sun."

"Hey, little girl," Bradley said with a sly wink, "who says you need sun to spread a little funshine?"

"First," said Gloria, "I'm not a little girl. Second, *funshine* isn't a word."

"You're right," said Bradley, still smiling (the way an alligator does before it chomps you in the butt). "Funshine is more of a feeling! Especially when you win big!"

Woo-hoo! I won enough coupons for a free pack of gum! It only cost two hundred dollars!

"Always remember one thing, kiddos," said Bradley. "Life's more fun after you've won. Hey, if you're not a winner, you're a loser—am I right?"

Gloria ignored him. She was looking for her dad.

"Is Manny Ortega still here?" she asked.

"Just left. You a fan?"

"Yes. I'm also his daughter."

Bradley raised his hand to slap her a high five. "Kudos on that, kiddo!"

Gloria left him hanging.

"Come on, P.T.," she said. "Let's head for home. I forgot to put on my funblock this morning. I think

I'm getting a really bad case of funburn."

We left without rolling a single wooden ball up a Skee-Ball ramp or checking out the Mega Mini indoor golf course.

Gloria didn't say a word as we crossed the parking lot and hit the sidewalk. I could tell she was doing some serious thinking. Finally, when we were maybe a block away from the Wonderland, she stopped in her tracks and turned to face me.

"We need to up our game, P.T.," she said. "Bigly."

Growth Hacking

"**W**hat we need is a growth hack," said Gloria as we headed for the Wonderland lobby to grab something cold to drink.

That's another great thing about living in a motel. The lobby's basically my living room except we have vending machines instead of fancy furniture with vinyl slipcovers.

"What's a growth hack?" I asked. "Is it like a growth spurt? I grew three inches this year. Grandpa says it's all the bologna he feeds me."

"A growth hack, P.T., is a process of rapid experimentation across marketing channels to identify the most effective ways to grow a business."

"Riiiight," I said, because I still had no idea what she was talking about.

I figured it was probably something pretty good,

though. Ever since Gloria and her dad had checked in, she'd been helping me come up with money-making schemes to keep the Wonderland afloat. Being an entrepreneur is sort of her hobby. She even plays the stock market, but only on paper. Last week, her make-believe portfolio was worth "a bajillion dollars and change."

If Gloria Ortega thought "growth hacking" was a good idea, I was all for it, whatever it was.

"Net-net, P.T.," she continued, "we need to generate new buzz and excitement around the Wonderland brand. Having the Twittleham Tiara on display gave us a nice bump, but now it's moved on to Cinderella Castle at Disney World."

I put my finger to my lips and urged Gloria to "ix-nay on the isney-Day," because I could see Grandpa in the lobby. My grandfather doesn't really like Disney World, because way back in 1970, Grandpa opened the Wonderland as a small family-run beachfront attraction known as Walt Wilkie's Wonder World.

Then, in 1971, the other Walt opened Disney World over in Orlando.

"The seventies were a great decade, P.T.," Grandpa always says. "For exactly one year."

Grandpa bopped the vending machine button that would deliver him a frosty can of Dr. Brown's

Cel-Ray soda. Yes, it tastes like carbonated celery juice.

We could also see Gloria's dad in the lobby. He was chatting with my mom.

I figured Mr. Ortega had swung by the motel after he wrapped up shooting his Fun Castle report. He probably needed to repolish his teeth.

By the way, I think my mom has something in common with our school bus driver: a serious crush on Mr. Ortega.

What does my father think about my mom flirting with the most handsome sportscaster on Tampa Bay TV?

Hard to say. Because I've never met the guy. I mean my father, not Mr. Ortega.

My dad left town before I was even born, and as far as I can tell, he's never come back.

But maybe someday he will.

Especially if Gloria and I come up with a super-incredible growth hack. Because when you're a big success, *everybody* wants to be your family.

Suite Dreams

Bells tinkled overhead as Gloria and I breezed through the lobby door.

"Hi, guys!" I said.

Mom and Mr. Ortega seemed to be in the middle of a super-serious conversation. I noticed a stack of glossy Fun Castle brochures sitting on the counter. Grandpa was flipping through them with one hand and holding a can of Dr. Brown's Cel-Ray soda in the other.

Grandpa belched. "Welcome home, kids," he said when his gas was all gone.

"Help yourself to soda, guys," said Mom.

She handed us a pair of dollar bills to feed into the vending machine's money-slurping slot.

"So, what do you think, Wanda?" Mr. Ortega asked Mom, picking up where they'd left off. "If I keep doing puff pieces like this feature about the Fun Castle, will the big dogs at ESPN ever take me seriously?"

Working for ESPN had always been Mr. Ortega's dream. It was why he'd kept moving around, hopping from channel to channel, city to city. He really wanted to impress whoever hired the on-air talent for the "Worldwide Leader in Sports."

"Well, Manny," said Mom, "I know *I* take you seriously. I even liked your story about the synchronized-swimming team at the Sarasota Senior Center."

"I appreciate that, Wanda. But I don't think I'm hitting it out of the park on a consistent basis."

Grandpa belched again.

This time the whole lobby smelled like salad that should've been refrigerated a month earlier.

"The Fun Castle looked pretty cool," I told Mr. Ortega, fanning the stinky air. "Gloria and I checked it out on the way home from school. Should make a good story."

"A lot of our guests went up there today," added Mom. "Gave them something to do during the day."

"What?" said Grandpa. "There's plenty to do here!"

"Well," I said, "I wasn't here to entertain them. Now, if you guys would just let me drop out of middle school . . ."

Mom arched an eyebrow unhappily. "Phineas Taylor Wilkie?"

Yep. Just like Mr. Frumpkes.

"So who's hungry?" blurted Grandpa. "Besides me, of course."

"I could eat," I said.

"Me too," said Mom, Gloria, and Mr. Ortega.

So we traipsed around back to the Banana Shack to see what Jimbo had on the grill.

Jimbo's our chef.

He's also the guy I used to think was my dad.

Our Own Personal Parrothead

Jimbo is what they call a Parrothead.

That means he loves the steel-drumming, guitar-strumming music of Jimmy Buffett. Jimbo is so laid-back I think he can sleep standing up.

Mom first met Jimbo when they worked together at a restaurant over in Orlando twelve or thirteen years ago. And since I'm twelve years old, that's just about all it took for me to decide that Jimbo was my dad.

Of course, I was wrong.

"Your mom and I are just good friends, man," Jimbo told me when I flat out asked him if he was my father. "Always have been. Always will be. So you want to, like, catch a wave later, man?"

That was basically the end of that.

Jimbo's Surf Monkey burgers are fantastic. And

he's elevated the Chunky Funky Monkey grilled cream cheese sandwich Gloria and I invented to new heights. (Who knew it needed a scoop of Cap'n Crunch cereal on top?)

Gloria and I grabbed stools at the bar. Mom, Mr. Ortega, and Grandpa shared a table.

"How's the stock market treating you, man?" Jimbo asked Gloria, even though she's a girl, because he calls everybody *man*.

"Fantastic," said Gloria. "On paper, anyway. The stocks I picked for my pretend portfolio are way up."

"Congratulations, man."

"Thank you," said Gloria. "But it's just pretend. It's not real."

"Maybe you should make it real," I suggested. "Just invest some *real* money in some *real* stocks."

"It's illegal, P.T. To purchase stocks on my own in the state of Florida, I'm pretty sure I need to be eighteen."

"Maybe your dad could do it for you," I told her. "Give him the money and let him buy the stocks."

"I'm kind of in a cash-poor position," said Gloria.

It was true. All the money we'd made selling souvenirs and putting on shows had gone straight into the Wonderland's bank account.

"Well," said Jimbo, "maybe your dad could do you a solid and front you. Give you what my aunt Lucille used to call a grubstake."

"Is that some sort of meat?" I asked.

"I don't think so," said Jimbo. "But I'd need to check my meat encyclopedia to be sure."

"A grubstake," explained Gloria, "is money furnished to an enterprise in return for a share of the resulting profits."

"There you go," said Jimbo. "That's probably what Aunt Lucille was talking about. Sometimes, with her, you couldn't really tell. . . ."

"Your dad has a steady salary at WTSP," I said. "Maybe he could—"

Just then Mr. Ortega sprang up and started doing some kind of raise-the-roof, potato-masher end-zone dance.

"Yesssss!" he shouted, showing Mom a text message on his phone. "There's an opening at ESPN!"

"That's great news, Manny," said Grandpa.

"Thanks, Walt," said Mr. Ortega. "But I don't have the job. Just a chance to *audition* for it. I'm going to need to polish up my demo reel. Invest in a new wardrobe. Maybe hire an audition coach. I might need new veneers for my teeth." He checked out his smile's reflection in a spoon. "Biff Billington has new veneers."

"Who's Biff Billington?" asked Grandpa.

"My main competition. Does the six o'clock sports out of Philly. The guy has one heckuva smile."

Grandpa shrugged. "You need new teeth, Manny, you can borrow mine. They're not even a year old. . . ."

He started reaching into his mouth. Mr. O quickly held up his hand.

"That's okay, Walt," said Mr. Ortega. "I'll call my tooth man. It'll definitely dent the ol' wallet, but maybe we can work out a payment plan."

I heard Gloria sigh beside me.

No way was she going to be able to borrow money from her dad to finance a real stock portfolio. Anything extra he might've had would now be going into his ESPN audition.

And even shinier teeth.

Hole in Fun

On Saturday, Gloria and I were hanging out at the Wonderland, playing a round of miniature golf on the Stinky Beard Putt-Putt course with our pals Bruce Brandow and Jack Alberto from school.

We were on hole six, the python.

"Aim at the right fang," said Jack, sounding sort of bored, "carom off the cheek, down the tube, out the back, bank off the tail curl, hole in one."

"But remember," I said, "this is no ordinary python."

"We know," said Bruce. "His name is Monty."

"And he came to earth on a flying saucer," said Jack.

"Because he likes Cheetos," said Bruce.

"Because he's curly," added Jack with a yawn. "Like a Cheeto."

I just smiled slightly. I figured I needed some new material. Maybe Bruce and Jack had both heard my statuary stories one too many times.

We know about Monty's rocket ship, too. It's powered by intergalactic Cheeto farts.

"Well played, Jack," said Gloria, keeping score on a pad with a stubby pencil. "You scored a hole in one."

"We all did," said Bruce.

"Because we've all played this course like fifteen million times," added Jack.

Just then, an airplane towing a banner advertising the Fun Castle's Mega Mini indoor golf course puttered across the sky.

"I hear the Fun Castle has, like, glow-in-the-dark monster holes," said Jack.

"And a fog machine plus all kinds of spooky music," added Bruce.

"I heard there's a half-price coupon in this week's *Beach Bargain Comber* magazine," said Gloria.

"Huh," said Jack. Then he checked the face of his phone. "Whoa. Look at the time. I gotta go. I promised my dad I'd help him do this thing."

"Me too," said Bruce.

They both took off running.

"I'll finish the round with you," said Gloria.

"Thanks."

We were about to tee up on hole seven, Seymour the Seasick Sea Turtle, when Grandpa ran onto the course, waving a letter.

"This is it, kids!" he shouted. "It's the break we've been waiting for all these years! If only your grandmother were here to see it, P.T.! She'd be spinning her Hula-Hoop like crazy!"

"What's going on?" I asked.

"We made it to the big time, kiddo! We're on the short list!"

Walt Versus Walt

"**A**nd here's the best part," said Grandpa between gasps for air. "Disney's kicked out of the competition this year!"

He was so excited he was hyperventilating. Gloria and I helped him sit down on a concrete alligator near Stinky Beard's treasure chest.

"What is it?" I asked.

Grandpa kept rambling and waving that sheet of paper. "All the big boys are officially eliminated. Disney, SeaWorld, Universal Studios, Busch Gardens—they're all out of the running. This is a once-in-a-lifetime opportunity, kids! My last chance to, finally, make all my dreams come true and show the whole world that Walt Wilkie is just as big a name as Walt Disney!"

I finally figured out what Grandpa was so excited about.

The letter he was waving around came from *Florida Fun in the Sun* magazine. Every year it sponsors a "Hottest Family Attraction in the Sunshine State" contest. Walt Disney World always wins. Except when Universal Studios, SeaWorld, or Busch Gardens does. Smaller attractions, like the Wonderland Motel, really don't stand much of a chance up against the big boys.

But it sounded like this year the magazine was shaking things up. The mega attractions were automatically eliminated. The contest would be focused on smaller places, like us!

"Oy," said Grandpa, taking off his golf cap so he could swipe away some of the sweat. "I need a Cel-Ray. Maybe a bag of Cheez-Its. My head is spinning. This is the biggest thing to happen to me since the day your grandmother and I opened up and stuck a striped straw into our first orange plastic ball filled with OJ."

"Let's go inside, where it's air-conditioned," I suggested.

Gloria and I each grabbed an elbow and escorted Grandpa into the lobby.

"Is everything okay?" asked Mom.

"Never better!" said Grandpa, triumphantly

bopping the soft drink machine in the sweet spot that magically made a Cel-Ray can drop into the bin—without feeding it any money.

"Dad?" said Mom from behind the counter. "You promised. No more free soda!"

"I'm cel-e-brating with Cel-Ray."

While Grandpa chugged his carbonated salad juice, I scanned the letter from *Florida Fun in the Sun*.

"This is awesome!" I said. "We really do have a chance!"

I passed the letter to Gloria.

"Definitely," she said after she read the first few paragraphs.

"What's going on, you guys?" asked Mom.

"*Florida Fun in the Sun* magazine has changed the rules for its 'Hottest Family Attraction' contest this year," I explained.

"The focus is on smaller attractions," added Gloria, who was still studying the letter.

"Disney's out!" hollered Grandpa. Then he burped. "Hip, hip, hooray! This is what I've been waiting for since 1971! A chance to show the world that Florida has two Walts in it!"

Actually, there were probably a lot of men named Walter living in the Sunshine State, but I understood Grandpa's point. Winning the contest would cool a nearly fifty-year-old burn and put Grandpa on equal footing with his longtime rival. Sort of. Well, at least he'd have a trophy that symbolically said that, for one brief shining moment, Walt Wilkie was just as important to Florida tourism as Walt Disney.

My grandfather, as you've probably figured out by now, is the most important man in my life. He's taught me so much—from how to swim to how to spin a story to how to toss a peanut into my mouth and never miss. I had to do everything I could to make my grandfather's biggest dream come true. We were not throwing away our shot. In my head, I heard triumphant music blaring. The kind of stuff they play in movies about scrappy boxers.

But then Gloria burst my bubble.

"Uh-oh," she said, turning the letter over and reading the stuff I'd skipped. "You guys didn't read all the fine print."

Making a Big To-Do

"They're looking for the best things *to do* with your kids in Florida," said Gloria, really stressing the "to do" bit.

"So?" said Grandpa, his mouth full of crushed Cheez-It crumbs. "There's plenty to do here! We've got the Stinky Beard Putt-Putt course. . . ."

Gloria and I looked at each other.

Jack and Bruce hadn't been too thrilled with their most recent round on the course.

"Then we have all the statues for people to gawk at," said Grandpa. "And Jimbo grills the best burgers on the beach. Plus, on weekends, you kids put on shows. Freddy the Frog karaoke. Behind-the-scenes movie tours. Treasure hunts—"

A guest came into the lobby and cut him off.

"Excuse me," said the man. "Do you folks have

any brochures for the Fun Castle? My kids saw that airplane with the banner and they're really looking for something fun to do this afternoon. . . ."

Mom smiled and handed him a glossy pamphlet from her stack on the counter.

"There's a coupon in the back," she said.

"Fantastic," said the man. "We've been here four days, and the kids are getting restless."

"Argh," said Grandpa, squinting like a pirate. "But have they tried Stinky Beard's Putt-Putt course?"

"Yes, sir. Six times."

"Hey," I said, thinking maybe if I spun a quick story, our goofy golf course would seem more exciting, "do your kids know that Stinky Beard was the smelliest pirate that ever sailed the seven seas? In fact, he smelled so bad that one time when he was sitting in the sand on the beach, a cat came along and buried him."

The man smiled. Politely.

"Cute story. Well, thanks again for the brochure."

He dashed out the door.

Because there wasn't enough *to do* at the Wonderland!

Mystery Shoppers

"Okay," I said. "I admit it. If we want to win, we have to up our game."

"Hang on," said Gloria, squinting at the letter again. "This year, *Florida Fun in the Sun* magazine has joined forces with TripsterTipster dot com."

"Hippy-dippy who?" asked Grandpa.

"It's a website and app, Dad," said Mom. "A lot of our guests make their reservations with it."

Grandpa swatted at the air. "App, schmapp. In my day, you took a reservation, you wrote it down on a three-by-five index card, and filed it in a tin box. Alphabetically!"

"Well, Dad, times have changed. . . ."

Gloria went back to reciting the rules. "There will be three rounds of judging. First comes the local competition. That would be us against everybody else who made the short list on St. Pete Beach. If we win, we move up to the Tampa Bay regionals. And if we win there, we're on our way to the Florida state finals."

"We have to win all three!" said Grandpa. "They only give us little guys a chance every fifty years. I may not even be here when they do it again fifty years from now!"

"Yes, you will," I said along with Gloria and Mom.

"You're right," said Grandpa, taking another swig from his soda can. "This Cel-Ray keeps me young. That Dr. Brown was a genius. Ten times better than Dr. Oz *or* Dr. Phil!"

"So how does the judging work?" asked Mom.

"Let's see," said Gloria, scanning the letter. "Okay. In approximately two weeks, a panel of three judges will schedule a visit to check out our top activities."

"You guys have a week off from school then," said Mom, checking the big family calendar she keeps behind the counter.

"Excellent," I said. "We'll put on our best shows ever that day."

"Wait," said Gloria. "There's more. 'Prior to the judges' visit, a mystery shopper will also visit your establishment.' Their vote will count for forty percent of our final score."

"What's a mystery shopper?" I asked, because it sounded like a spy heading into Walmart to buy invisible ink.

"A mystery shopper is typically a person employed to pose as a customer in order to evaluate the quality of customer service," Gloria explained.

"When do they show up?" I asked.

"Anytime."

"How do you know it's them?"

"You don't. That's the mystery."

"Seriously? Could they be here already?"

Gloria shook her head. "No. This says the undercover critic will 'visit your attraction sometime during the two-week period between your receipt of this letter and the official visit by the panel of judges.'"

"When did you receive the letter?" I asked Grandpa.

"Just now. Gus the mail carrier handed it to me. Plus a whole stack of catalogs. Why does this Eddie Bauer fellow think I need a puffy parka? This is Florida, not Oregon!"

We all just nodded. Sometimes Grandpa veers off topic.

"Mom?" I said. "We need to keep an eye on every new guest who shows up during the next fourteen days. One of them could be our mystery shopper."

"Should I ask them when they check in?" she wondered.

"Bad idea, Ms. Wilkie," said Gloria. "Mystery shoppers prefer to remain anonymous."

"Right. Gotcha."

Just then, as if on cue, the phone rang. Mom answered it and took down a new reservation. The second she hung up, the phone rang again. Mom took *another* reservation.

Coincidence? I sure didn't think so.

"Booyah!" I shouted. "One of those two new reservations has to be our mystery shopper! They both called right after we officially received our letter. The mail carrier probably texted the magazine."

"Maybe," said Mom, sounding super skeptical. She does that sometimes.

"Who are we competing against?" I asked Gloria.

"Let's see." She found the list. "Here we go. The top family-fun attractions in St. Pete Beach are: Captain Sharktooth's Pirate Cruise, fishing off the pier at John's Pass, the Wonderland Motel—"

"Woo-hoo!" shouted Grandpa. "U-S-A! U-S-A!"

When he was done fist pumping, Gloria read on.

"Splash Down Water Park at the Seawinds Resort . . ."

"Ooh," I said accidentally. "That place is awesome."

Grandpa shot me a look.

"Sorry," I said.

He waved his hand at me. "Don't worry. We'll add a Slip 'N Slide—roll it out near the dolphin fountain. You kids can make up a story about how slippery dolphin spit is. The Seawinds won't stand a chance."

Big, Bold, Boffo

"Who else made the short list?" asked Mom.

"Fort De Soto," said Gloria.

"Bor-ring!" said Grandpa. "It's a state park."

"A very beautiful state park," said Mom.

"Well, good thing this isn't a beauty pageant," said Grandpa. "Anybody else?"

"Just one more," Gloria told him. "The Fun Castle on Gulf Boulevard."

"What?" I said. "They're brand-new. They just opened."

"They were probably grandfathered in," said Grandpa, which made me smile (because he's my grandfather). "They're new here on St. Pete Beach, but everybody already knows what they have to offer, because they've had a place over in Tampa for years. It doesn't matter. We're gonna win, baby, win! Right, P.T.?"

I looked at Grandpa, and for maybe the first time in my life, I was speechless.

I didn't want to let him down.

I also didn't want to see him get hurt.

"Well," I said, "we definitely *could* win. . . ."

"Uh-uh-uh. Don't 'could' on me, kid. Employ the power of positive thinking. If you can dream it, you can do it."

Gloria nodded. "That sounds like something Walt Disney probably said."

"He might've said it first, but I'm saying it now, because I dream when I'm not even sleeping. The Wonderland is going to win this contest. I guarantee it!"

I had never heard Grandpa sound so stoked about anything, except, maybe, his ride-along railroad, which he had shut down in the 1980s and still hoped to bring back "one day soon."

"But to win, we need to think big," he said, rubbing his hands together. "We need to think bold. We need something boffo." He snapped his fingers. "Theme rooms!"

"What?" said Mom.

"Tell me: What's the most popular room on the property?"

"Easy," I said. "The Cassie McGinty Suite."

That was a suite of rooms on the second floor where the famous movie star had stayed while filming *Beach Party Surf Monkey* at the Wonderland. The walls were decorated with movie posters and paraphernalia. It was like the Hard Rock Cafe, except with surfboards and movie props instead of electric guitars and Kiss costumes.

"Correctomundo!" said Grandpa. "So here's my big new boffo idea: We remodel a few rooms. Turn them into theme rooms. Make it fun to go to bed. For instance, how about the Banana Cream Pie Room? It'll be based on the Banana Shack's most popular dessert, complete with piecrust crown molding, a whipped-cream ceiling, a circular bed in a pie-pan frame, and dollops-of-cream pillows!"

"Won't that cost a lot of money?" asked Mom.

"Probably," said Grandpa. "But it will be worth every penny. You know why, Wanda? You gotta spend money to make money!"

Now you can have your pie and sleep in it, too!

The Banana Cream Pie Room

Muggy with a Chance
of Brainstorms

"Ooh," said Grandpa, "I got another one."

He held up both hands to frame his vision.

"The Mermaid Room. It'll be like sleeping underwater, but without the drowning."

There'd be an aquarium in the shower, and you'd sleep in a clamshell bed. The pillows? They're shaped like pearls!

"Remind me," said Grandpa. "When are these judges coming?"

"Two. Weeks." Gloria, Mom, and I said it all together.

Grandpa nodded. "And the mystery shopper person?"

"When are those two new reservations coming?" I asked Mom.

"Next Friday," said Mom. "Both of them."

"Oh, boy," said Grandpa. "I need to call Billy. Pronto!"

"Who's Billy?" asked Mom.

"A contractor my buddy Johnny Adamo recommended. Room 106 is vacant. It'd make a great pie room."

"But we're being judged on *activities,* Grandpa, not rooms," I said. "We need to come up with fun things for people *to do.*"

"You ever sleep in a banana cream pie? What could be more fun than that?"

"But only one family will be able to enjoy the theme room," said Gloria. "We should also focus on activities for all our guests."

"Fine," said Grandpa. "We'll upgrade the shuffle-board court."

"Seriously?" I said. "Shuffleboard is boring."

"And," added Gloria, "it's also for old people. No offense."

"None taken," said Grandpa. "Fine. Forget shuffle-board. Come up with a new idea, kids. Something hip and trendy. I can't do all the brainstorming around here. It'll give me heartburn."

"Well, maybe we could put in a Spikeball set," I suggested.

"It's the hottest new beach and backyard game, according to the *Today* show," said Gloria. "And, of course, Mark Cuban loved it on *Shark Tank*."

"What is it?" asked Mom.

"You bounce a ball off a Hula-Hoop-sized net," I said. "Your opponent bounces it back."

"If they miss," said Gloria, "you score. It's like beach volleyball with a trampoline instead of a net."

"And," I said, snapping my fingers the way Grandpa does when he's having a big idea, "we could add a bunch of mini trampolines so the players can bounce around, too!"

"Boom!" said Grandpa. "Keep 'em coming, kids! I'm gonna go call Billy! He needs to start whipping up plaster for the Banana Cream Pie Room ceiling!"

Grandpa was so happy he practically skipped out of the lobby.

"We should probably check out the other attractions on the short list," suggested Gloria. "Try to hone our competitive edge. Don't forget, prestigious awards can do more to boost top-line sales than almost any other PR vehicle."

"Besides," I added, "Grandpa is pumped."

"You guys?" said Mom.

"Yeah?"

"Thanks."

"For what?" asked Gloria.

"Making Dad so happy."

"Well," I said, "let's just hope we can actually win this thing for him."

"Of course we can," said Mom. "We've got a secret weapon: you two!"

Sheesh, I thought. *Not like there's any pressure or anything.*

Stiff Competition

Gloria and I headed out into the sunshine. It was so muggy my eyeballs fogged up.

"Is your dad home?" I asked.

"He's up in his room," said Gloria. "Editing his demo reel."

"He knows a lot about the activities in the area."

"True. He's done stories for WTSP on just about all the attractions on the short list."

We bounded up the stairs to the second floor and went to Mr. Ortega's room. He was hunched over his laptop, watching video clips of himself.

"Dad?" said Gloria.

"One second, hon." He clicked his computer mouse. "Just need to shave off a few more frames. This is that story I did about high school football championships where they dumped the bucket of

Gatorade on my head. This is going to be the tightest demo reel in the history of ESPN auditions."

"Will that help you win the job?" I asked.

"I sure hope so, P.T.," said Mr. Ortega. "Because, as the legendary football coach Vince Lombardi once said, 'If it doesn't matter who wins or loses, then why do they keep score?'"

"So the scoreboard operator has a job?"

"Good point, P.T. Good point. Now how can I help you kids?"

We gave him a quick recap of the revamped *Florida Fun in the Sun* competition and ran down the list of our competitors in the first round.

Mr. Ortega whistled.

"They've all got great work ethics and will definitely come to play," he said, because sports reporters say stuff like that all the time. "Let's break it down. Fishing off the pier at John's Pass? Just about as boring as it sounds. Unless you love bait buckets full of live, squiggly shrimp."

"No thanks," I said. "I like mine deep-fried with tartar sauce."

"Fort De Soto? Beautiful. Nice nature hikes. Excellent bird-watching. But there hasn't been much real action there since they stopped firing the cannons."

He liked Splash Down Water Park at the Sea-winds Resort.

"They'll have a real shot at winning this thing," he said.

"What if we put in a Slip 'N Slide?" I asked.

He looked at me. "Like I said, they'll have a real shot at winning this thing."

"So how about Captain Sharktooth's Pirate Cruise?" asked Gloria.

"Never heard of that one," said Mr. Ortega. "Must've flown under my radar."

"Then there's the new Fun Castle," I said.

"The big kahuna," said Mr. Ortega. "They've got major marketing muscle and state-of-the-art electronic gaming action. Defeating them will definitely be a challenge."

That made me gulp a little.

"Did you see their Mega Mini indoor golf course when you did that story?" I asked.

"Yes. And I have to report it is more amazing than anything you might imagine. It features fluorescent holes glowing under ultraviolet lights. They've got smoke machines. Sound effects. Animatronic figures like sharks with snapping jaws. They're hitting on all cylinders, guys, and have taken miniature golf to the next level—the mega mode!"

It almost sounded like his voice was in an echo chamber when he said that last bit.

"We definitely need to scout them out," said Gloria. "And Captain Sharktooth's. See what we're up against."

"Where first?" I asked.

"Captain Sharktooth's," said Gloria. "Because we know absolutely nothing about their operation."

● ● ●

Bright and early Sunday, we biked over to the pirate cruise's pier. They already had a sign up saying they were on the short list for *Florida Fun in the Sun*'s hottest family attraction.

"Note to self," said Gloria, speaking into her phone. "Make short-list sign."

We bought tickets and boarded the ship.

Then we both froze in our tracks.

Because you'll never guess who Captain Sharktooth's weekend tour guide was.

Boring, Boring, over the Bounding Main

"**W**hat are you two doing here?" asked the tour guide, who was wearing one of those corny captain hats.

It was Mr. Frumpkes. Our history teacher.

"We just thought we'd check out Captain Sharktooth's Pirate Cruise," I said, trying not to laugh. Mr. Frumpkes was also wearing white shoes, white pants, white gloves, a blue blazer with frilly gold trim on the sleeves, and a snazzy bow tie. He looked ridiculous.

"Are you Captain Sharktooth?" Gloria asked innocently.

"No!" snapped Mr. Frumpkes. "It's my weekend job, Ms. Ortega!" He thrust out his gloved hand. "Do you have tickets?"

Belay those cookies, youngster. Chips Ahoy! have nothing to do with sailing.

"Aye, aye, Captain," I said, and handed him our cardboard stubs.

"Then welcome aboard. And, Mr. Wilkie?"

"Yes, sir?"

"This is an educational tour. We'll have none of your shenanigans. Do I make myself clear?"

"Yes, sir."

We found a spot along the starboard railing as the boat shoved off. The cruise wasn't very crowded. Maybe four families.

"Parents?" Mr. Frumpkes said into a microphone. "Make certain you keep your children under control at all times. They're your responsibility on weekends, not mine! Now then, if you look over the sides of the boat, you may see some fish. This is the Gulf of Mexico. It is full of fish. And kelp."

"Are we going to attack a boat or something?" asked one kid.

"Why on earth would we want to do that?" asked Mr. Frumpkes, wrinkling up his nose.

"Because we be pirates!" hollered the boy. "Arrrrgh!"

"You're using improper grammar, young man. Mom and Dad? You should keep an eye on that. Now then, John's Pass, where we were docked, was named after John Levique, a sea turtle farmer in the 1800s. . . ."

And blah-blah-blah.

Something about gold and buried treasure and the "Great Gale of 1848."

To be honest, it had all the makings of an awesome story. But in Mr. Frumpkes's hands, it was totally boring. Fact: how you tell a story is just as important as what it's about.

The kids on the ship looked miserable.

Especially one boy in glasses. He had a crew cut, jug-handle ears, and a very green face. I thought he was getting sick—and not just from Mr. Frumpkes's blah-blah-blahing.

"I don't feel so good," he told Mr. Frumpkes.

"You are most likely experiencing a form of

motion sickness characterized by a feeling of nausea."

The boy urped. "Yes, sir."

"That's because your brain is receiving conflicting signals. While your eyes show you a world that is still, the equilibrium sensors located in your ears are sending signals that the environment is in motion. . . ."

The more Mr. Frumpkes laid out the scientific details of seasickness, the more kids started feeling woozy. Pretty soon, all the boys and girls on the boat (except Gloria and me) clasped their hands over their mouths and moved closer to the railings.

They were all about to start chumming the water with chunks of vomit!

All Hands on Deck!

I could tell the kid in the glasses was about to hurl.

"Don't you dare vomit on our hardwood deck, young man," scolded Mr. Frumpkes.

I leapt into action.

"Ahoy, mateys," I hollered to all the seasick kids in my best Stinky Beard pirate voice. "Look ye to the horizon!"

"Mr. Wilkie?" said Mr. Frumpkes, scowling at me. "What exactly do you think you're doing?"

"Saving your hardwood deck, sir."

That startled him enough that I was able to grab the microphone out of his hand.

"I know me an old pirate trick," I said. "Whenever I feel a wee bit queasy on the poop deck because I had cackle fruit for breakfast . . ."

"Those are eggs," translated Gloria.

"Aye! When my stomach feels like it might scuttle me into a 'thar he blows' situation, I simply look at the horizon! Try it. As we head back to port, look out into the Gulf and stare at the horizon until your world feels fixed and horizontal, which, by the way, is why they call it the horizon and not the vertic-izon."

A couple of kids laughed. They were already feeling better.

"This is how the famous pirate Jean Le Bigfeet sailed from France to Florida."

Mr. Frumpkes was fuming. "Do you mean Jean Laffite, the French-American privateer?"

"Nargh. Jean Le Big-feet was bigger than Jean Laffite. He set sail from France after eating a really big French dinner. French fries. French toast. One of those French dip sandwiches. As he crossed the Atlantic, he would've totally lost his lunch, but fortunately, he was

Sacré bleu! I believe I ate too many chocolate croissants and snails with garlic butter.

sailing with the world-renowned French physician and puke-ologist, Dr. Le Barf.

"He was the world's leading expert on seasickness and said, '*Fromage, mon capitaine.* Look to zee horizon!' Jean Le Bigfeet did as the doctor instructed, and safely sailed all the way to Florida and John's Pass, where he stole all of that turtle farmer's gold!"

The passengers were still staring at the horizon when we docked and tied off at John's Pass. No one barfed, hurled, yakked, or ralphed.

Gloria and I scampered down the gangplank to the dock before Mr. Frumpkes could write us up a detention slip, which, technically, he probably couldn't do, because we weren't at school, but we didn't want to risk it.

Funmeister Misery

Gloria and I grabbed some conch fritters at Crabby Bill's.

They weren't as good as Jimbo's.

"We are so going to win this thing," I said. "That pirate cruise was so bad it made everybody sick to their stomachs."

"We still need to defeat the Fun Castle," she reminded me.

"So let's go check them out."

Gloria and I biked over to the Fun Castle.

We paid for a pair of putters so we could scope out the Mega Mini indoor golf course. Our clothes and teeth were glowing. The Fun Castle had an awful lot of ultraviolet lights in the ceiling.

We were on number three, the King Kong hole, where you had to shoot your ball through the hairy legs of a giant animatronic ape with banana breath who was beating his chest and roaring.

We saw that "funmeister" Bradley coaching a kid.

"What's your name, son?"

"Um, Dill."

"Like the pickle?"

"Yes, sir."

"Not many pro golfers named Dill."

"No, sir."

"Not many Olympic athletes or all-star quarterbacks, either."

"You're correct, sir."

"Well, Dill, you need to push yourself. You need to give me one hundred and ten percent."

"But that's mathematically impossible, sir. . . ."

Bradley didn't like hearing that. His face turned orangish, which is what I think happens to red under ultraviolet light.

I recognized Dill. He was the same little guy in glasses we'd met on Captain Sharktooth's Pirate Cruise. The first one to almost hurl.

Winning isn't everything, Dill. It's the only thing!

Uh-oh. I'm feeling seasick again.

"Hey, Dill!" I shouted as if we were old pals. "Why don't you play with us instead of Bradley?"

"If he plays with me," shouted Bradley, "he can learn what it takes to be a winner."

"You could probably become a winner with us," I said.

"We're both terrible," added Gloria. "You're practically guaranteed a victory."

"I don't even know which end of this shiny stick to use," I said, waving my putter around.

"But I've already played the King Kong hole," said Dill.

"So?" I said. "Play it again. You'll get a better score because you know how to beat the big ape."

When I said that, I was sort of looking at Bradley, who was glaring back at me.

"What's your name, son?"

"P. T. Wilkie," I told Bradley.

"That's a weird name."

"True. But it's also very easy to memorize."

"So?"

"So memorize it," I told him. "Because you're going to see it engraved on a trophy when me and my friends at the Wonderland Motel beat you in the *Florida Fun in the Sun* contest."

Now I really, really, *really* wanted to win.

And not just for Grandpa.

Now I wanted to beat funmeister Bradley, too.

Duuude

Gloria and I headed back to the Wonderland and decided to hit the beach, which is basically our backyard.

On our way down to the surf with our boogie boards, we bumped into a total surfer dude who was setting up shop maybe ten yards away from our rear retaining wall. He had long sun-bleached blond hair, a smudge of white zinc on the tip of his snout, way cool shades, and one of those puka shell necklaces people wear in Hawaii.

"Howzit, brah and sistah?" he said when he saw us. "The surf was epic today. Fully macking, man. The waves were total corduroy, y'know?"

"Sure," I said.

"I guess," said Gloria.

The guy had all sorts of rentable beach gear set

up around a trio of bright blue umbrellas (which you could also rent). We're talking kayaks, surfboards, beach bikes, kites, stand-up paddleboards, skimboards, and a stack of beach chairs. A sign stuck out of the sand: Beach Bum's Equipment Rentals.

The guy told us his name was Corky.

"I'm P. T. Wilkie," I said. "This is my best friend and business partner, Gloria Ortega."

"Howzit?" said Corky.

"Fine," said Gloria. "I guess. Um, may I ask a question?"

"Fer shure, dudette."

"Is it your intention to set up shop here behind the Wonderland Motel on a regular basis?"

"Maybe. Who's asking?"

"Me and P.T."

"What? You dudes have something against life, liberty, and the pursuit of happiness?"

"Hardly," said Gloria. "In fact, we embrace and celebrate the American free enterprise system."

"We're also looking to up the number of activities available to our guests," I added. "You're right behind our motel. The Wonderland."

"Therefore," said Gloria, "we might find some seriously sustainable synergies."

Corky crinkled his zinc-painted nose in confusion. "Huh?"

"We might be able to work together," I said. "We send you guests, you give them something fun to do."

"Sounds like a plan, little man," said Corky.

He shot out his hand to shake on the deal.

I stroked my chin.

"What's the problem, brah?"

"How do we know if your gear is any good?"

"Easy, dudes. Test it out."

And that's exactly what Gloria and I did. For maybe three hours. For free.

I think that's why they call it the *free* enterprise system.

Biz Wiz

When we were done having fun in the sun, we headed back to the Wonderland.

Mom and Grandpa were in the lobby, going over sketches for the Mermaid Room. Apparently, construction was already under way in the Banana Cream Pie Room.

"Billy just finished the whipped-cream ceiling!" said Grandpa. "It looks so good I almost licked it."

"Oh," said Mom, "I almost forgot. I heard from *Florida Fun in the Sun* magazine." She consulted a pink notepad. "Our official panel of judges will be here two weeks from Tuesday. That'll be the Tuesday of your vacation week."

"Great," I said. "We have plenty of time to prep some new shows. We've already lined up a bunch of new beach activities."

"Really?" said Mom. "How?"

"We worked out a strategic alliance with a freelance equipment-rental agent," said Gloria.

"A guy named Corky," I said. "He set up shop out back on the beach. He has a ton of cool stuff. Everything from boogie boards to sun umbrellas."

"Working synergistically," said Gloria, "we will be able to exponentially maximize the Wonderland's fun-in-the-sun quotient."

Grandpa and Mom had blank looks on their faces but nodded anyway.

"Gloria?" said Grandpa.

"Yes, sir?"

"Can I be honest with you?"

"Of course."

"I don't understand half of what you say. But I don't need to. You're a wiz, kid! You still do that mock stock portfolio thing you do?"

"Yes, sir."

"You still winning?"

"Yes."

"She's a bajillionaire," I added.

Gloria blushed. "Only on paper."

"Well," said Grandpa, rubbing his hands together, "we need to turn your paper profits into real moola-boola to help finance all these instant improvements we're making around here. I want to build a spaceship room, too. The bed is an Apollo space capsule. The lamps look like rockets. The TV plays nothing but *Star Wars* and *Star Trek* DVDs. I also have an idea for an Orange Juice Room. Everything's orange—and there's an extra spigot on the sinks for OJ. But to pull off all this redecorating, we're gonna need some major bucks. We're gonna need *you*, Miss Ortega."

22

Grubstake

"**B**-b-but . . . ," Gloria protested.

Grandpa held up his hand.

Gloria quit sputtering.

"Gloria," said Grandpa, "I'm going to give you a grubstake."

"Really?" said Mom. "How?"

"Easy. I've been saving my pocket change for years. I have fifteen half-gallon orange juice bottles filled with coins. Pennies, nickels, dimes, quarters—even some of those Susan B. Anthony silver dollars you don't see anymore."

FRESH-SQUEEZED COINS! CHA-CHING!

"Tomorrow," he said, "I'm taking all fifteen jugs down to the bank, dumping those coins into that counting machine they've got, and then I'm taking Gloria and the money to my good friend Laurette."

"Who?" asked Mom.

"Laurette Oldewurtel. She's a stockbroker. Used to come here when she was a kid and count the seashells in the parking lot."

"Oh, right," said Mom. "Laurette . . ."

"You'd take all that money and invest in my stock picks, Mr. Wilkie?" said Gloria.

"You bet. You're a winner, kid. A winner!"

When Gloria heard that, she ran across the room and hugged Grandpa.

I did, too.

The Babysitters Club

"Oh, I almost forgot," said Mom when the hug-fest was over. "We just had a check-in. A family of three. You need to take their bags to their room ASAP, P.T."

She gestured to a pile of suitcases stacked on a rolling cart.

"Any chance they're our mystery shoppers?" I asked.

"I don't think so. They made their reservation weeks ago."

Since I'm the closest thing the Wonderland has to a bellhop, I rolled the newly arrived family's luggage to a room on the first floor.

A boy opened the door.

"Hi, again!"

It was that kid Dill.

"Mom? Dad?" he called over his shoulder. "The bags are here."

"Great."

I wanted to make double-triple sure that Dill's parents weren't our mystery shoppers.

"So," I said, "you folks here to have some *fun in the sun*?" I winked to see if they'd wink back.

They didn't.

"Not really," said his mom. "Too much work to do."

"We'll be indoors mostly," said his dad. "As long as the AC works, we're happy."

"Is there room service?" asked his mom.

"Yes, ma'am," I told her.

"Perfect. We may never have to leave the room."

Dill's mother and father quickly unpacked their twin laptop computers, asked me for the Wi-Fi code (it's GRAPEFRUIT123), and sat down at the desk to start clacking keys.

"Have fun, son," they said to Dill.

"Will do," he said back.

Then he turned and smiled at me.

Like he wanted somebody to play with.

"So," I said, because I felt sorry for the guy. "You should definitely hit the pool. It's a blast."

"Cool," said Dill. "Let's go!"

"Um, do you want to change into your swimsuit first?"

"Already wearing it."

"Oh."

"Hey, it's Florida? Am I right?"

"Riiiight."

To be perfectly honest, I had never once thought about wearing a swimsuit all day. And I live in Florida.

We left the room and headed for the pool.

"Maybe your mom and dad will come out for a dip later."

"No way," said Dill. "They're super-busy e-commerce entrepreneurs. Their idea of a fantastic family vacation is an air-conditioned room with high-speed Internet at a motel with a babysitter for me."

When Dill said that babysitter bit, he was smiling straight at me.

The Fountain of Tall

The next week at school, fired up by Grandpa's faith in Gloria (he had five thousand dollars in those coin jars!), I wrote a new show during my free periods.

All the best amusement parks have shows: Disney World, Universal Studios, even Weeki Wachee Springs, where the mermaids put on (what else?) *The Little Mermaid.*

I called my new script "Ponce de León Discovers the Fountain of Tall."

We'd already painted our twenty-five-foot-tall Muffler Man statue (a molded fiberglass giant Grandpa had bought from a tire-repair shop in Michigan back in the 1990s) to look like Ponce de León, the famous explorer my middle school is named after.

As you may not know, because you don't go to my

middle school, Ponce de León spent years searching for the Fountain of Youth—magical waters that would totally reverse the aging process way faster than all those makeup ads promise on TV. But I digress.

With the help of Gloria and her friends in the Junior Achievement club at school, we'd already put a new spin on the old legend. We said that Ponce de León never had found the Fountain of Youth but he had stumbled across the Fountain of Tall, right here on St. Pete Beach. That's why our twenty-five-foot-tall statue of Señor de León is "life-size."

The Junior Achievement kids helped us design and market Ponce de León water bottles, which we fill from our motel's magical fountain (also known as Grandpa's garden hose) and sell for five dollars. Most buyers do it as a joke, the same way some tourists buy invisible-dog leashes when they're on vacation.

Now, with the help of another friend from school, Lily Lawler, we were ready to take the Fountain of Tall to the next level. Literally. Because Lily, an eighth grader, is six and a half feet tall. I kid you not. Her last growth spurt had a growth spurt.

Plus she has a Mini-Me little sister in fifth grade named Matilda Lawler, who looks exactly like her.

If we were going to be judged on our activities and entertainment options, we needed new shows.

Maybe even a magic show with one funny trick!

Waterworks

On Thursday we were stoked.

First we learned that Grandpa's five-thousand-dollar investment in Gloria's stock picks was suddenly worth *twenty* thousand dollars.

The theme rooms were fully financed.

Grandpa called Gloria a genius. They celebrated with Dr. Brown sodas. Cel-Ray for Grandpa. Black cherry for Gloria.

Then we put on our brand-new Ponce de León pageant during the dinner rush at the Banana Shack. I wanted to try it out in front of an audience before our prime mystery shopper suspects checked in the next day.

We had maybe a hundred spectators.

"Ladies and gentlemen, boys and girls," I said into the microphone we'd rigged up, "welcome to the Wonderland Motel, where there are always marvels to behold and stories to be told. Tonight's marvel? The Fountain of Tall Extravaganza!"

We didn't have a fog machine like the Fun Castle to make everything look super spooky, but Jimbo hooked up a couple of fans and blew the smoke from his burger grill our way. When it hit the colored floodlights beaming up from the ground, the effect was awesome.

In the concession stand (it was Mom's card table with a pink-flamingo tablecloth), Gloria and her Junior Achievement sales team were standing by with crates of Ponce de León bottled water for sale.

After my opening rap number, I launched into the amazing tale of the conquistador's quest for the Fountain of Youth.

Ponce hunted for gold
in Puerto Rico,
found himself a parrot
and named him Chico.

"They never found it," I said. "Probably because, like all conquistadors, he never bothered to ask the locals for directions. However, Señor de León did accidentally discover the legendary Fountain of Tall!"

I pointed to our swimming pool.

"See that dolphin spewing crystal-clear water? That astonishing elixir is bubbling up, straight from the source. Of course, the chlorine in the pool cuts down on the water's magical properties, so don't worry, you won't go swimming and come out too tall for your swimsuit."

"Ha!" honked Dill, seated in the front row. "Hilarious!"

Now it was time for the fun twist, because like they say, every story needs a beginning, a middle, and a twist.

"But don't take my word for it. I have a bottle of water taken directly from the Fountain of Tall with nothing added to dilute its oomph. That bottle is sitting on a table behind this life-size statue of Ponce de León. Who would like to see the magical marvel at work?"

Everyone clapped.

"Very well. I need a volunteer from the audience."

Dozens of arms shot up.

I, of course, picked Lily Lawler's little sister, Matilda.

"You there. In the front row. Yes, you. Head on back and take a swig. See what happens."

"You bet!" said Matilda, because she'd memorized her line.

She scampered behind the statue.

We heard some very loud glugging.

And six-and-a-half-foot-tall Lily Lawler came out.

The crowd cracked up.

After the show, Gloria and her friends sold a ton of molded water bottles.

"This will make a great gag gift," I heard one happy customer say with a laugh.

"I'll take six!" said another.

"I need a dozen," said Dill. "What can I say? I'm short."

Within fifteen minutes, the bottles were sold out.

The show was a hit! The souvenir merchandise was a hit! People were having fun in the sun, even though, technically, the sun was starting to set.

We were definitely on our way to winning Grandpa his trophy.

But then I heard another customer.

He wasn't so happy.

"How'd you clowns even make the short list? This place is a joke." He slapped a finger-and-thumb *L* on his forehead. "Loser."

It was Bradley.

The funmeister from the Fun Castle.

Playing the Market

"**I** want to beat those Fun Castle guys so bad," I told Gloria in the cafeteria the next day.

Everybody else loved our Ponce de León show, and we had completely sold out our water bottles, but all I remembered was Bradley calling me a loser and the Wonderland a joke.

"I think we have a very good chance," said Gloria. "Your grandfather has spent the week cooking up even more amazing ideas for theme rooms."

"Really? He didn't tell me about them. . . ."

"That's because you're not the one picking securities to finance the venture."

"True. So, what does he want to build next?"

"A game room."

"We already have a game room."

"This would be a room that looks like one of

those wacky Lemoncello board games your grand-father always wins when we do game night. You have to solve puzzles and go on a scavenger hunt to find the shampoo and toilet paper."

"A room like that would cost a fortune!" I said.

"Well, P.T., as your grandfather said, it takes money to make money. That's why he and I are talking to Ms. Oldewurtel this afternoon."

"But you'll be back home by three, right? It's Friday. Those two guests are checking in *today.* The ones who mysteriously made their reservations minutes after we received the letter about the competition. We need to work undercover in the lobby. Scope out which one is our mystery shopper."

"I'll be back in plenty of time. Your grandfather's picking me up right after lunch. Mr. Sharp, my math teacher, signed a permission slip for early dismissal. He thinks, win or lose, this stock market enterprise will be a very educational experience."

"Have you made your stock picks?"

"Yes." Gloria pulled out the three-ring binder she used to track what she called her mock stock portfolio. There were all sorts of newspapers and magazines only adults read stuffed into the cover pockets. Junk like the *Wall Street Journal,* the *Financial Times,* and something called *Barron's,* which I guess you read if you want to become rich enough to be a baron.

"I'm focusing on fast-growth stocks," said Gloria. "And a few companies nobody else is looking at because they don't have what I call the kid's-eye view of the market or a nose for the next high-flying fad."

"What've you got?"

"I'm intrigued by this one company that makes pencil toppers you can chew and blow bubbles with. One, shaped like a slice of pizza, also tastes like pizza."

"Snackable school supplies. That'd be great, especially if you have a late lunch."

"Exactly. Sure, the risk in all my picks will be a little higher than most investors are comfortable with, but greater risk can mean greater reward. Plus, we're looking for a super-quick payday. Your grandfather is spending money like mad, fixing up all these theme rooms."

So now the pressure was on Gloria, too.

She had to turn her make-believe profits into real money. Fast.

● ● ●

We reconnected at three o'clock sharp in the lobby.

Mom was behind the counter, twisting a pencil in her hair because she was nervous about our mystery guests, too. Gloria and I sat, as nonchalantly as possible, on the wicker sofa near the postcard rack.

"Did you buy the edible eraser company stock?" I asked.

Gloria nodded. "Definitely. They just signed a deal

with Jelly Belly. The new eraser flavors should be phenomenal."

"Now what happens?"

"We wait."

"For the stock to go up?"

"Hopefully."

Yeah, I guess I forgot that part. What goes up can also go down.

Mystery Guests Sign In?

At three-fifteen p.m., neither of our prime suspects had arrived in the lobby.

But Dill did.

"What're you guys doing?"

"Nothing," I said.

Gloria said, "Reading magazines," which was probably a better answer.

"Those are from, like, last Christmas," remarked Dill.

"Never too early to find a new cookie recipe," I said.

"Cool," said Dill. "Can I hang with you guys?"

I almost said, "No. We're too busy spying." But I caught myself.

"Sure."

Dill grabbed a wrinkled *Sports Illustrated*.

"Awesome. A preview of last year's Super Bowl. I already know who wins!"

Gloria and I raised our magazines and peered over the tops—just like we'd seen undercover espionage agents do in movies. Dill, of course, copied our moves.

Finally, someone came into the lobby to register: a very athletic middle-aged guy (probably as old as Mom and Mr. Ortega) in a baseball cap, a jogging shirt, shorts, and flip-flops.

His luggage? A bunch of duffel bags, stuffed to the max. He had a small notebook jammed into the back pocket of his high-tech shorts. He looked like the kind of guy who'd go to football games and shout "woo-hoo" a lot.

Right behind athletic Mr. Jim Nasium (well, that was the name I made up for him) came a woman with her son, who I pegged to be a second or third grader. They were wearing matchy-matchy outfits and looked like something out of a resort-wear catalog. They had two small rolling carry-on suitcases. Ms. Matchy-Matchy kept looking around the lobby, checking everything out.

Secretly, we both love to go shopping.

Did she just call herself a mystery shopper???

I figured Mom had pegged Ms. Matchy-Matchy to be our mystery shopper. That was probably why she gave her and her son the newly renovated Mermaid Room.

Jim Nasium, our other leading contender, got the Banana Cream Pie Room—complete with a coupon for a free slice of banana cream pie at the Banana Shack.

"Fine," said the guy. "I've always wanted to sleep in a high-calorie, high-fat dessert."

Unlike Ms. Matchy-Matchy, he didn't want any help taking his bags to his room.

Did that mean *he* was our mystery shopper?

He might've been afraid we'd see some top secret judge stuff in his luggage. Or read his notes on that notepad in his pocket!

"It has to be one of them," I whispered to Gloria.

"But which one?" Gloria whispered back.

"Why are you guys whispering?" whispered Dill.

"It's a secret," I told him.

"Awesome. I love secrets!"

Me too. But I loved secret mystery shoppers even more. Especially if one of them helped us win this thing for Grandpa.

Our First Intern

Dill struck me as super lonely.

You probably know the type. The new kid at school. The girl sitting all by herself in the cafeteria. The boy nobody wants when choosing up sides for volleyball. The kid who doesn't see too many other kids his own age because his parents are so busy tapping their computer keys that they don't take the time to organize family activities.

I guess you could say I have a soft spot for lonely kids.

After I took Ms. Matchy-Matchy's bags up to her room, I saw Dill sitting by the pool. He had his head in his hands and heaved a sad sigh.

"Hiya, Dill," I said cheerily.

"Hey."

Gloria came down the steps from the second floor, peeling a tangerine.

"We need to start wowing those two new arrivals, ASAP," she said.

"How come?" asked Dill.

"Because, Dill," I said, "here at the Wonderland, we like to wow *all* our guests! And to do that, we might need your help."

Dill instantly perked up. "Really?"

"Yep. I'm thinking we should add you to our fun-in-the-sun entertainment crew."

"Great idea," said Gloria. "Dill can be our intern."

"What's an intern?" asked Dill.

"Someone who learns a lot," I said, "and has a ton of fun doing wacky stunts and shows with us."

"Awesome!"

"Plus, you don't get paid," added Gloria.

"That's so cool!" said Dill.

"First job," I said, "sampling one of Chef Jimbo's Surf Monkey burgers." I led the way to the Banana Shack.

Dill crinkled his nose. "Is it made out of monkey meat? Is this like an initiation test?"

Gloria shook her head. "I keep telling Jimbo he needs to change that name. It sends the wrong message."

"It sounds like it's made out of monkey meat," said Dill.

"It isn't, man," said Jimbo, slapping three softball-sized globs of chopped beef onto the griddle. "You want monkey tail fries?"

"Are *those* made out of monkey?" asked Dill.

"No way, man," said Jimbo. "Our fries are totally vegan, because potatoes are, like, a vegetable."

While we waited for our food, Gloria and I filled Dill in on some of his duties.

I pointed to our frog slide. "We could use you the next time we do a Freddy the Frog karaoke show."

"Okay. What do I do?"

"Sing along with the frog. Be the first one up when I ask for a volunteer."

In showbiz lingo, Dill was going to be my shill—a pretend customer to encourage other folks to play along.

As Jimbo served us our burgers and fries, I saw movement to our left. The athletic guy came out of the Banana Cream Pie Room in his bathing suit.

"Eat fast," I said to Gloria and Dill. "It's showtime. Jimbo? Can I borrow your walkie-talkie?"

He slid it down the bar.

I pushed the talk button. "Grandpa? Do you have your ears on?"

"Ten-four, good buddy," he crackled in reply.

"Grab your microphone. We need to do a Freddy show."

"But those are only on weekends."

"This is a special command performance. For Jim Nasium."

"What? Who's he?"

"One of our prime suspects."

Grandpa didn't answer right away. Finally, he said, "For the thing with the thing?"

"Exactly!"

"Give me ten seconds to fire up the amplifier."

"You got it."

"What's going on?" asked Dill.

I gestured toward the man who'd just spread out a pool towel on a lounge chair. "We're going to show that guy that nobody has fun-in-the-sun activities like we do! Nobody!"

Croaking Like a Frog

With Dill's help, Grandpa and I launched into a primo Freddy the Frog poolside performance.

"That's just a frog slide," said Dill, doing his lines beautifully. "It can't talk or sing."

"Well, my friend," I said, "that's where you're wrong."

The guy we needed to wow put down his *Florida Fun in the Sun* magazine.

Aha! I knew he was our mystery shopper.

He started paying attention to the show. So did everybody else hanging around the pool.

"Freddy doesn't move around much. He thinks nobody can see him if he stays perfectly still."

"I'm like butter on a hot toasted bagel," boomed Grandpa's frog voice from the speaker we'd hidden inside the slide's mouth. "I'm blending in here."

"That frog's not really talking," said Dill, just like I had instructed him to. "That's a prerecorded tape."

"Is that so?" growled Grandpa. "Then how come I can see your glasses and your red swimsuit?"

After a few jokes, it was time for the main event: Croaky Karaoke, which was what we called singing along with Freddy.

Every time we did it, folks loved it.

Grandpa, Dill, and I launched into one of our biggest hits, "Jeremiah Was a Bullfrog."

The kids at the pool were cracking up.

So were their parents.

But our prime suspect wasn't.

Jim Nasium was shaking his head.

I mimed slicing my throat with my finger. Grandpa killed the music.

Gloria was off her barstool fast.

"Is there some problem, sir?" she asked the man who just might be our undercover critic.

"You bet there is. I came here for outdoor activities, not corny kiddie shows and karaoke."

I hustled over to help Gloria. Dill hustled over behind me.

"Sir, may I ask you your name?" I said.

"Nick Cerone."

"Well, Mr. Cerone, you are in the right place. How'd you like to kitesurf against the Dolphin King?"

Both eyebrows went up behind his sunglasses.

I had his attention.

"That sounds awesome!" said Dill.

Yes, I had *his* attention, too.

Where Pelicans Soar

As the four of us hiked down to the beach, I quickly re-spun the story I'd told in Mr. Frumpkes's class.

"The other day, Mr. Cerone, I was carving across a wave. Totally cranking. It was epic. All of a sudden, out of nowhere, this dolphin pops up! He challenges me to a race."

"The dolphin talked?" he asked skeptically.

"He didn't need to. I could read the challenge in his eyes. I could hear it in his taunting squeaks and mocking cackles."

"So what'd you do?"

"I whipped out a kite, slipped on a harness, gripped my board with my toes, and took off. Before long, I was soaring across the water, leaving that dolphin to chase my shadow, because I was flying high—up where pelicans swoop. One of *them* wanted to race me, too, so I said, 'You're on.' I left that pelican eating my exhaust fumes, mostly because he had a huge fish flopping around in that pouch thing they have for a chin. It was totally slowing him down."

You know why the pelican was kicked out of the motel?

He had a huuuuuge bill.

Fact: when you go back and retell a tale, you'll always find room for improvement. Like they say, there's no such thing as good writing, only good rewriting.

"You beat the pelican *and* the dolphin?" asked Mr. Cerone with an easy grin.

I nodded. "A sea turtle and a manatee, too. And so will you, sir, after we hook you up with the proper gear."

"Can I get some gear, too?" asked Dill.

"Sure," I told him. "But you might want to start out with a boogie board."

"I did that the other day," said Gloria. "It was a blast."

"Wanna race?" said Dill.

"Sure," said Gloria.

We took Mr. Cerone and Dill down to Beach Bum's Equipment Rentals.

The surfer dude, Corky, was chilling in a low-slung chair under one of the bright blue umbrellas. He had even more stuff for rent than he'd had the other day, including a trio of paddleboats shaped like flamingos.

"Hey, Corky," I said, "we'd like the Wonderland discount for some of our new guests."

"Excellent, little dude. Waves are awesome today. I did an el rollo before I ate it on a gnarly heavy." He stood up and wiped the sand off a board. "You ready to hit the surf, brah?"

"Can I get a kite and harness, too?" asked Mr. Cerone.

"Fer shure. I can definitely hook you up."

"I might also want to do a little sea kayaking."

"At the same time?"

"No. Afterward."

"Oh. Okay. That'll work."

Corky helped Mr. Cerone into his rig.

"Now this is what I call a great setup," Mr. Cerone said. "All these fun beach activities, right in your own backyard."

"Well, sir," I said, "when it comes to fun in the sun, we aim on being number one and never outdone." I was rhyming out slogans like crazy. I think I could have a career in advertising someday.

Mr. Cerone took off in a kitesurfing getup and hit the waves.

When he caught the wind and was airborne, Gloria and I turned to each other and hollered, "Booyah!"

We'd just wowed our first potential mystery shopper.

Fun in the Sun

Mr. Cerone flew over the Gulf.

Then he kayaked.

Then he skimboarded across the slick sand and flung a Frisbee and played beach volleyball and read a paperback novel that Corky also had for rent.

"Nothin' but beach reads," the surfer dude said proudly. "True page-turners, brah."

Mr. Cerone did more beach activities in two hours than most people do in two weeks.

While he was having fun, renting everything Corky had to offer, Gloria, Dill, and I piled into those flamingo-pink paddleboats and played salt-water bumper cars, a game we sort of made up as we went along.

Dill giggled so much I thought he might pee in his pants. Not that anyone would notice. That's another great thing about playing in the Gulf of Mexico: when nature calls, you are free to pee. Hey, do you think all those fish out there wait until they find a bathroom to relieve themselves?

When we finally headed back to the Wonderland, Mr. Cerone thanked us for a "great day" and went to the Banana Shack to "grab a burger."

Score some more points for the home team. I knew he'd love his dinner, too.

Dill went to his room.

Gloria and I headed into the lobby, where her father was showing Mom something on his phone.

"It's a Twitter war!" Mr. Ortega said. "Biff Billington up in Philadelphia just hashtagged 'ESPNlock.' He thinks he's a shoo-in for the job because he landed a major one-on-one interview with the one and only Phillie Phanatic."

So when your belly swings right, that's a yes?

"That big furry green bird thing?" said Mom.

Mr. O nodded. "Arguably the most recognizable mascot in all of North American sports!"

I raised my hand.

"Yes, P.T.?" said Mr. Ortega.

"Does the Phillie Phanatic ever actually talk? Doesn't he just, like, dance and wiggle and wave and stuff?"

"Exactly! That's why this interview is such a major get! It'll all be done without saying a word.

"I don't know how I'm going to beat that," said Mr. Ortega, shaking his head.

"Easy," I said. "Interview somebody even more interesting. Maybe somebody who actually talks."

Mr. Ortega snapped his fingers. "That's genius! P.T.? You just hit it out of the park."

"Thanks."

"I've been hearing about a golf prodigy over in Clearwater," said Mr. Ortega. "A kid named Johnny Zeng. He's never done a TV interview. His parents are trying to protect him from the harsh spotlight of fame. He's only sixteen, but the PGA is considering bending the rules and letting him turn pro. He'd be a huge get. My sources tell me Johnny Z could become the youngest player to ever win a major championship."

I grinned.

Because Gloria and I were kind of like Johnny Zeng. We might become the youngest players to ever win a very major tourist-attraction trophy.

Surf Bored

I was up bright and early Saturday.

Mostly because that's when Jimbo makes his famous Chunky Monkey Chocolaty Peanut-Buttery Flapjacks: a stack of chocolate chip pancakes smothered in melted peanut butter (instead of syrup) and topped with crumbled chunks of Reese's Peanut Butter Cups. That'll get your motor running.

Gloria and Dill joined me at the Banana Shack. Gloria went with Jimbo's Pineapple Paradise pancakes—topped with tropical fruit and coconut. Dill chose the Good Morning Sunshine special. Jimbo makes them with banana-blueberry eyeballs, a blackberry nose, sliced-strawberry sunbeams, and a raspberry-syrup smile.

When we were almost finished with our breakfasts, mystery shopper suspect number two, the

Oh, boy. He's going to slice and bite me. Yippee!

woman we'd dubbed Ms. Matchy-Matchy, came down to the pool with her son.

"I am soooo bored," I heard the boy moan. "There's nothing to do here."

"Well, just play in the pool for a little while," suggested the mom. "This afternoon, we can go someplace with more activities. Like the Seawinds Resort or the Fun Castle. I need to check those out for work, too."

Uh-oh.

That was not good.

The mother definitely sounded like she was an undercover judge. She had literally said she needed to check out our competitors "for work." If she was grading us on fun things to do, the worst thing in the world would be for her son to be bored out of his gourd.

Pirate Schemes

"**W**e need to fix that," I whispered to Gloria.

The boy was pouting.

"He looks so sad," said Dill. "He should order some happy-face pancakes."

"I could take her a menu," said Gloria. "Pretend I'm a server . . ."

I shook my head. "No. We need something bigger than Jimbo's pancakes."

"Really?" said Dill. "Because these things are the size of a tricycle tire. . . ."

I snapped my fingers.

"Remember all those pirate costumes and eye patches and junk we bought for the Pirate Chest Treasure Quest promotion when you first moved in?"

Gloria nodded. "Sure."

"All that stuff's still stored in Grandpa's work-shop," I said. "We should call a few friends. Invite them to come over and play pirate. I'll run across the street to Shore Enuff Stuff and buy some squirt guns. Maybe one of those water cannons."

"May I ask a question?" said Gloria.

"Go for it."

"Why?"

"Years ago," I told her, "Grandpa used to have a ride-along railroad that chugged in a loop through the parking lot. We need to borrow a page from his playbook."

"Was your grandfather a football star?" asked Dill.

"Nope," I said. "He was, and still is, a master showman. Back in the day, when kids started getting bored puttering around in his choo-choo, he'd hit them with a plot twist: bandits! Guys in cowboy hats and robber masks would hold up the train. Grandpa would deputize everybody on board, pin tin stars on their chests, and pass out the cap guns, and together they'd send those bad guys packing."

"So we're going to stage a train robbery?" asked Gloria.

"Nope. A pirate attack!"

Pirates, Yo-Ho-Ho!

We divided up the tasks.

Or as Gloria put it in business lingo, we "peanut-buttered" them out.

She called the Alberto brothers, Jack and Nate; plus Bruce Brandow; super-tall Lily Lawler; her sister, Matilda; and six other pals from school.

Meanwhile, Dill tagged along with me.

We raced across the street to Shore Enuff Stuff and bought a bunch of pirate flintlock water pistols, a couple of Tampa Bay Buccaneers pirate flags, some inflatable pirate swords, and a Super Soaker Hydro Cannon.

"That looks like it's from outer space," said Dill when he saw the high-tech water squirter.

"Excellent idea!" I said. "The Wonderland will

be the first motel on St. Pete Beach ever attacked by space pirates! To the costume aisle, Dill!"

Shore Enuff Stuff had everything. Toys, games, books, even goofy dress-up costumes.

"Some of our pirates should wear light-up deely boppers on their heads," I told Dill, "so they can look like they came from outer space! We need to grab some balloons, too."

"Woo-hoo!" squealed Dill as we careened our cart through the store and loaded up. "I hoped there'd be balloons!"

We made our purchases and carried four shopping bags bulging with more than enuff stuff back across the street. We met Gloria and the gang in Grandpa's workshop, told everybody the plan, and started getting dressed and ready for our first-ever Pirates from Outer Space Extravaganza.

Grandpa came in when we were all dressed up and ready to go. Half of us were wearing deely boppers; half of us weren't. We needed to look like two opposing teams, because when you're telling a story, you need conflict or nothing too exciting is ever going to happen.

Grandpa placed his hand on my shoulder and smiled.

"You have learned well, grasshopper," he said. (I'm not exactly sure why.) "Now go out there and give them the old razzle-dazzle!"

Pirates from Outer Space!

The matchy-matchy family was still poolside.

But now the boy's pout was on its way to the meltdown/tantrum zone.

So squirt guns blazing, deely boppers bopping, we attacked the pool, pretending to be two bands of pirates, fighting each other.

Jack and Nate Alberto led the alien team. They were whacking Bruce with an inflatable pirate sword the size of a caveman's club. Dill was waving a Tampa Bay Buccaneers flag.

"You've got to help us," I said to Ms. Matchy-Matchy's son, who stopped whining when Jack slammed me with a blast from his water cannon.

"Why should I help you?" he asked.

"Because we're the good guys."

"You look like a pirate."

"True. But I'm a Tampa Bay Buccaneer."

"We're locals!" shouted Dill. He waved the football team's flag higher.

Jack super-soaked me again. Right in the face.

I gurgled. Pretended like I was wounded. Like I couldn't fight on.

"Here," I said, reaching into my pirate coat. "Take this. Fight back."

It was a water balloon.
The boy heaved it at Jack.
I handed him another one.
He walloped Nate.
"You're my hero," I told him—right before I dramatically died and fell into the pool.

As the "bad guys" reeled from the boy's water-balloon barrage and, one by one, toppled into the pool, I heard him cry out, "Mom, this is the most fun I've ever had anywhere!"

"Booyah!" Gloria and I hollered, and knocked knuckles.

Because we'd just wowed the second leading suspect for our mystery shopper.

We were one step closer to making Grandpa's lifelong dream come true.

I was busy giving everybody a high five when I heard some unpleasant puttering overhead.

Two planes.

Each one hauling another Fun Castle banner.

VISIT THE FUN CASTLE, WHERE FUN RULES!

NOW WITH DAILY PIRATE ATTACKS!

GULP!

?

Checking Out

On Sunday, both Mr. Cerone and Ms. Matchy-Matchy checked out.

Gloria and I were sitting on the wicker sofa in the lobby again, pretending to read ancient magazines so we could eavesdrop on our departing guests' final words.

"We wish you could've stayed with us longer," said Mom as she printed out Mr. Cerone's final bill.

"Me too. You guys have a great setup here. All that beach gear for rent out back? Fantastic! And that Banana Cream Pie Room? Delicious. The whole room smells like a tropical breeze."

Fact: air fresheners come in a Hawaiian Aloha scent. Grandpa bought a case of the stuff for the Banana Cream Pie Room.

"I'll definitely be coming back," said Mr. Cerone as Mom handed him his receipt.

If he was our mystery shopper, we were golden.

Ms. Matchy-Matchy and her son came to the lobby about ten minutes later.

"I hope you enjoyed your time at the Wonderland," said Mom as the printer churned out another receipt.

"We certainly did!" gushed Ms. Matchy-Matchy.

"I wish we could stay longer!" said her son. "That pirate show was awesome! And the pillows in the Mermaid Room sparkle like seashells."

Ms. Matchy-Matchy smiled. "I found the bubbler in the aquarium to be quite soothing. Almost hypnotic. I slept like a baby."

"I'll tell my father," said Mom. "The bubbles were his idea."

"We have a few other places in St. Pete Beach we need to check out," said Ms. Matchy-Matchy, sounding more and more like a mystery shopper. "But we'll definitely be coming back."

She and her son left.

I leapt up and did a happy dance.

"We are so going to win this thing!" I said as I boogied in place with shoulder shrugs, arm rolls, and hip sways.

That was when Mr. Ortega walked into the lobby.

"Smooth moves, P.T.," he said. "Reminds me of

the Ickey Shuffle, an end-zone dance made popular in the late eighties by Cincinnati Bengals fullback Elbert 'Ickey' Woods."

"You guys did a fantastic job," said Mom. "We might actually have a shot at winning this thing. Your grandfather will be so happy, P.T."

That made me blush a little, so Mom turned the spotlight back to Mr. Ortega.

"How's your audition for ESPN going, Manny?"

"Still playing catch-up with Biff Billington and the Phillie Phanatic. But I'm sending out feelers, trying to land a one-on-one interview with Johnny Zeng. I hope his parents say yes. Right now, I'm on the dance floor but a long way from the band."

"Huh?" said Gloria.

"I'm working on my golf clichés," her dad explained. "That one means I'm on the green but far from the stick."

"What's the stick?" I asked.

"That flag thingy they put in the hole."

"Oh. Cool."

"Wish me luck, all. And remember—you chip for show, you putt for dough!" He gave us a two-finger salute off the edge of his eyebrow. "Be the ball!"

Be the ball? Why would anybody want to do that? When you're a golf ball, people whack you with fourteen different kinds of clubs.

Wait! It's me! P.T.! I'm being the ball!

AAAIIIEEEE!

We all smiled and nodded even though we were totally confused. We were new to golf lingo, too.

Gloria and I headed out of the office.

And bumped into Mr. Frumpkes.

He was carrying a shrink-wrapped stack of shiny brochures for Captain Sharktooth's Pirate Cruise.

"Put these in your lobby," he barked, the same way he orders me to keep my eyes on my reading material when I get bored in history class and start looking around, wondering what if George Washington's army had had just one fighter jet. Or a tank. *What if?* is where a lot of good stories get started. Daydreams, too.

"Um, we're competing against your pirate cruise, remember?" said Gloria.

"So? I'm your teacher. I know what's best."

"Then why are you wearing that shirt?" I cracked.

"Because the fabric is very breathable. It also wicks away my moisture. I have very active sweat glands."

Whoa. TMI.

I took the stack of brochures from Mr. Frumpkes, mostly because it's what merchants do up and down St. Pete Beach. We help each other out—even if we're competing for the same prize. Also because I didn't want to hear any more about Mr. Frumpkes's overactive sweat glands.

Gloria and I traipsed back into the lobby and put the pirate cruise pamphlets in the brochure rack. Mr. Frumpkes watched us through the floor-to-ceiling windows. He tapped on the glass when he thought we weren't giving him a primo slot.

So we swapped the Captain Sharktooth's Pirate Cruise leaflets with the ones for the Sea Horse BBQ Grill in the top row. Mr. Frumpkes gave us a semi-satisfied "that's better" harrumph and moved up the block.

"The coast is clear," I said when I couldn't see him anymore.

Gloria and I went outside.

And this time, we bumped into Dill.

"Hi, guys," he said, waving at us eagerly, even though we were only two feet away. "What are we gonna do today?"

"We're not sure," I said. "But, I was thinking,

maybe we should go scout out the Seawinds Resort. See what else they've got that we don't."

"A jet pack," said Dill.

"Excuse me?"

"A jet pack! It's amazing. You put on a helmet, blast off, and fly over the ocean."

Okay. This we had to see.

And then we had to see if we could somehow copy it.

Rocketing into the Future

Dill led the way when we reached the resort, which was only about ten blocks down Gulf Boulevard from the Wonderland.

The place was huge, with all sorts of things to do.

"But the BlastOff is the best!" said Dill. "You're like a jet pilot without a jet, just the engine!"

We hurried down a winding path, through all sorts of tropical landscaping, to the beach and what the brochures called the "coolest, most exhilarating water sports ride of your life—guaranteed to take your beach vacation to new heights."

It was incredible.

We watched a guy and girl ready to blast off.

They were waist-deep in the water, wearing helmets, life vests, and jet packs. Each backpack was hooked up to a thirty-foot-long fire hose connected to a floating water pump.

"Blast off!" shouted the ride operator.

Foamy white water shot out of two nozzles on each jet pack, rocketing the guy and girl twenty feet up to the sky. It was amazing.

Okay. That is the coolest thing I have ever seen in my life. And I live in a motel.

I had to try it.

Fortunately, I was tall enough to ride this ride.

Gloria paid for my ticket; Grandpa had given her a credit card linked to her portfolio. That was a good thing. Because one jet-pack ticket cost—hang on to your swimsuit—ninety-nine dollars!

"It's a jet pack," said the guy in a Seawinds polo shirt who swiped her credit card. "Jet packs are expensive. We have to import them from the future."

"It's also a legitimate business expense," said Gloria. "Research."

"I want to ride, too," said Dill. "I brought my own money."

"I don't know," I said.

"I'm tall enough. I wanna do it. Please?"

Dill was giving me his sad puppy dog eyes.

Who can resist the sad puppy dog eyes?

Having a Blast?

The guy running the ride noted the wad of cash in Dill's hand and cut him some slack, pretending not to see him going up on tippy-toes to meet the minimum height requirement.

"You two flying together?" he asked.

"Yeah," I said.

"I'm just watching," said Gloria.

"Costs ten dollars to watch," said the guy.

Gloria rolled her eyes and slapped a Hamilton into his gimme-gimme hand.

Dill and I strapped on our helmets, life vests, and harnesses. The ride operator gave us, like, a five-minute training talk.

"Don't do anything stupid," were his closing remarks.

And then it was time to blast off.

He fired up the two supercharged water pumps. Water shot up the six-inch-wide fire hoses and sprayed out the one-inch-wide nozzles. You don't need to be a physics genius to figure out what kind of pressure that's going to create. White clouds, as thick as booster-rocket fumes, zoomed down and smacked the water we were wading in. For every action, there is an equal and opposite reaction. We lifted off! I was actually flying, just like I said I had in all those kitesurfing stories.

I was ten, twenty, thirty feet up. The brochure was correct. My beach experience had definitely reached new *heights*.

WOO-HOO!

I can fly. Now I just hope I can land.

Unfortunately, Dill's liftoff wasn't quite as smooth.

Have you ever seen a garden hose go wild, whipping around on the ground, when you accidentally dropped it?

That's kind of what happened to Dill.

He was too tiny. He was off-balance. He was panicking.

And I couldn't blame him.

He skittered along, slapped the crest of the waves, and bounced around on his belly like a flat rock you skim across a lake.

"Hey, kid!" the ride operator shouted at Dill. "You break it, you buy it!"

"I-I-I c-c-can't c-c-control this c-c-crazy thing!" shrieked Dill.

"Hang on!" I shouted. "I'm coming."

I eased up on my throttle, dipped down, swerved behind Dill, and grabbed him under the arms.

That meant I had let go of my control handles.

Now I was the out-of-control garden hose.

We both went spinning. Sideways.

We totally wiped out.

Good thing we were flying over the Gulf of Mexico.

When you crash on water, it doesn't hurt as much as it would on land. But it really, really stings.

"You okay?" I asked Dill when we both bobbed to the surface and spit out some seaweed we'd recently swallowed.

"Yes. I think so. But, P.T.?"

"Yeah?"

"Can we go back to the Wonderland and play pirates? It didn't hurt so much."

"Good idea."

This is NOT fun in the sun!

Because we're going to crash in the water!

We're in the Money

Monday, Gloria and I went back to school and the stock market reopened.

I mention that last bit because Gloria checked some stock-tracker app on her phone during lunch and shouted, "Woo-hoo!"

It was her turn to do a happy dance.

Apparently, that edible-eraser company's stock had just split. That didn't mean it had broken in half or gotten up and walked away. It meant that every single share of stock Gloria and Grandpa held in the company had, magically, become *two* shares of stock—and the price per share was skyrocketing! We could afford all of Grandpa's wacky ideas. We could afford a second swimming pool.

"The stock split coupled with the jump in share price over the past week means we've quadrupled our investment," Gloria explained. "Your grand-father can afford his third and fourth theme rooms."

"Does he have ideas for the new rooms?"

Gloria nodded. "The Bat Cave."

"Cool."

"And the Bologna on White Bread Room."

"Huh?"

"The bed is shaped like a sandwich. The blankets are pink and spongy. The pillows are pickles."

"What about the mustard and American cheese?"

"Yellow and orange sheets."

For the first time in forever, we had all the money we needed to do just about anything we wanted to do.

Now you can have my favorite lunch even when you're asleep!

Now all we needed was a winning idea. Pickle pillows were cool, but they weren't technically family activities—unless you and your kids used them for a pillow fight.

After school, Gloria ran up to her room, because she wanted to check the day's "volatility and volume" and see if she could do any "bottom-fishing before the closing bell."

I still had no idea what she was talking about.

I drifted down to the beach to think.

We'd done well with the mystery shoppers. But the panel of judges, accounting for 60 percent of our *Florida Fun in the Sun* score, would arrive next Tuesday.

What could I do, in just seven days, to create an attraction so amazing it would guarantee Grandpa the prize he'd been chasing for over two decades?

I didn't have a clue.

Until the answer hit me.

Seriously. It hit me in the side of the head.

Some people on the beach were playing Frisbee. The wind knocked their disc off course, and it whacked me, right above the ear.

When I was done saying "ouch" and rubbing my ear, I remembered something another bud at school, Kip Rand, had told me a few months earlier.

"Frolf."

Of course. Frolf was the answer!

Frolf!

Frolf is a quicker way of saying "Frisbee golf."

Or what is known in professional circles (yes, there are professional Frolfers) as disc golf. You aim your disc at a target—usually a pole with loops of dangling chains—and try to park that disc in the basket below.

HOW TO FROLF in 3 easy steps!

FLING THE DISC.

HIT THE POLE AND CHAINS.

LAND DISC IN BASKET. (REPEAT 17 TIMES.)

Way back before Spring Break, Kip Rand had told me, "You guys could lay out an insane Frolf course on your property!"

He was right!

We could use all of Grandpa's wacky statues for holes. Dino the Dinosaur. Morty D. Mouse with his humongous cheese wedge. The rocket ship. Even Ponce de León, the Muffler Man.

That night, over dinner at the Banana Shack, I told everybody my idea.

"I love it!" said Grandpa.

"It sounds like fun," added Mom.

"We could definitely monetize it," said Gloria.

We all stared at her.

"That means we could make money doing it," she explained.

"Ohhhh," we all said together.

"We should do a Surf Monkey hole," I said.

Gloria agreed. "That'll help us boost sales of movie souvenir merch."

"And we could put a sand castle hole, with the world's toughest sand trap, down on the beach," I said.

"You kids could do that Fountain of Tall gag with your friend at the Ponce de León statue," said Mom, getting in on the action.

"Brilliant, Wanda!" said Mr. Ortega. "Your brain is as beautiful as your, uh, the rest of you!"

"Why, thank you, Manny," said Mom.

I was jotting down everybody's ideas on the back of a Wonderland postcard.

"This is great, you guys. Now we just have to build it!"

"And I need to build my bologna sandwich room!" added Grandpa.

"We only have seven days to build it all," said Gloria. "The judges will be here a week from tomorrow."

"So hey, hey, Tampa Bay," said Mr. Ortega, giving us his TV catchphrase, "it's time to get to it!"

Game On!

We worked on our Frolf course every chance we had for the rest of the week and into the weekend.

Grandpa and his contractor finished four more theme rooms in record time.

Monday we started our vacation from school and opened the Frolf course to our guests.

They loved it!

Especially the zip line we rigged down to the eighteenth hole on the beach. It was like riding a golf cart to chase after your first shot, only way more fun.

Tuesday afternoon, right on schedule, the panel of judges from *Florida Fun in the Sun* magazine showed up. Ms. Matchy-Matchy, the woman who'd stayed with her son in the Mermaid Room, was one of the judges.

Woo-hoo!

We'd guessed correctly! She had to be our mystery shopper.

"Good to see you again," I said.

"Is this new?" she asked, looking at all the happy Frolfers flinging discs and rattling chains on hole poles.

"Yes, ma'am," I said. "Here at the Wonderland, we're always adding fun new *activities.* Enjoy!"

Gloria and I teed off in a Frolf foursome with Dill and Ms. Matchy-Matchy's son, whose name, we learned, was Geoffrey.

Dill was surprisingly good at Frolf. On the jackalope hole, he ricocheted his disc off our outdoor soda machine to avoid the palm tree blocking his straight-line shot.

"Woo-hoo!" Dill hollered when he pinged another hole in one.

His grin was wider than the jackalope's.

But Geoffrey, the judge's son?

He wasn't smiling so much.

Zipping Up a Win

Geoffrey was also extremely excellent at disc golf.

In fact, after sixteen holes, he and Dill were tied.

"I got lucky," said Dill, penciling in another "1" on the scorecard for the jackalope hole.

"Maybe I'll get lucky, too," said Geoffrey.

He took his shot—copying the one Dill had just made.

"Nailed it!" he shouted.

"Way to go!" said Dill, who was a superb sport.

"Did you put down my hole in one on the score-card?" demanded Geoffrey.

"Of course."

"Let me see."

Dill showed him the card.

While Geoffrey made certain that Dill had properly recorded his hole in one, Gloria looked at me. I could read her eyes: she did not like the judge's bratty little son.

Neither did I. But I knew we had to let Geoffrey win. If he did, he'd tell his mother what a wonderful, fun-in-the-sun time he'd just had.

If he didn't, he'd whine to Mommy and we'd probably be eliminated from the competition in the first round.

We moved on to the eighteenth hole—the sand castle down on the beach. The tee box was near the clothes-drying pole anchoring the zip line ride.

"You guys go ahead," I said to Gloria and Geoffrey. "I want to show Dill something."

"What?" asked Gloria.

I gestured toward the pool. "The, uh, dolphin fountain."

"Oh, I've already seen it," said Dill.

"But I want to show you something special."

Gloria narrowed her eyes. She seemed to know what I was about to do.

"Show Geoffrey how to use the zip line," I told her.

Gloria did.

But she wasn't happy about it.

Winner Takes All

Dill and I slipped over to the pool, where the gurgling fountain would cover up what I was about to say.

"Dill?"

"Yeah?"

"I have to ask a huge favor."

"Anything. After all, you saved my life at the Seawinds."

"Okay. I need you to take a dive."

"In the pool? Right now? I thought we were playing Frolf. . . ."

"It's an expression. It means you throw the game. You lose on purpose."

"Why?"

"So Geoffrey leaves happy."

"Is he sad?"

"Not right now. But I think he will be if he loses."

"You're probably right. He seems supercompetitive. Me? If I have fun, then I've won."

I clapped him on the shoulder. "Good attitude."

"Thanks. And don't worry. I'll make it look like I was really trying to win."

"Thanks, Dill."

We headed back to the tee box.

Gloria shot first. Her disc twirled about ten feet and died in the sand.

Dill went next.

He did something with his follow-through that made the Frisbee hang in the air, where a breeze sent it sailing sideways.

"Oh, man," he moaned. "That wind came out of nowhere!"

"Better luck next time," said Geoffrey with an evil grin. "Oh, there is no next time. This is the final hole."

He let his disc fly.

It whirled like a ninja star, banged the pole, rattled the chains, and fell into the basket.

"Nailed it!" Geoffrey shouted. "Another hole in one!"

"Wow," I said through a forced smile. "You won. Congratulations, Geoffrey."

"Losers!" He ran off to tell his mother about his triumph.

Dill shook my hand. "Thanks for another awesome afternoon, P.T.! You too, Gloria. I'm going to go buy a ton of souvenirs so I can always remember just how much fun I had playing Frolf with you guys!"

He took off.

It was just me and Gloria, standing at the end of the zip line, not saying a word.

Finally, Gloria shook her head.

"I am so disappointed in you, Phineas Taylor Wilkie. Dill deserved to win. Or at least have a chance at winning."

"Sorry," I said. "But it's best for the motel. Geoffrey's mom's a judge. A judge *and* our mystery shopper!"

"You don't know that for certain."

"No. But I have a pretty strong hunch."

◦ ◦ ◦

Turned out my hunch had been a good one.

Bright and early the next morning, Mom got a call from the magazine people.

We'd won the first round.

We were voted the top family activity attraction on St. Pete Beach. We'd beaten the Fun Castle, the Seawinds, and everybody else, including Mr. Frumpkes and Captain Sharktooth's Pirate Cruise.

When we heard the news, Grandpa took us

Florida *Fun* IN THE *Sun* magazine

THE WONDERLAND WINS ON ST. PETE BEACH!

FROLF COURSE IS PURE FUN IN THE SUN

"MY SON GEOFFREY WON TOO" — says happy mom

CEL-RAY SODA

into his workshop to show us four square inches of dusty, uncluttered shelf space.

"That's the spot! Right there is where I've always planned on putting whatever trophy I won when I beat Disney. Thanks to you two, I'm getting closer to filling it!"

It was on to Tampa and the regionals!

And if I had anything to do with it, we were going to win that round for Grandpa, too. He was finally, after forty-some years, going to bring home a trophy for that empty spot on his shelf.

They're Baaaaack

That morning, the TripsterTipster website listed all the attractions moving on to the Tampa Bay regional round of the competition.

My jaw dropped. It does that sometimes when I'm surprised.

Something called the Super Fun Castle was in the regionals, too.

"I thought we already beat those guys!" I said as Gloria and I stared at the list.

"The Super is their Tampa location," said Gloria.

"Fine," I said. "We beat them once, we can beat them again."

Gloria clacked a couple of keys on the computer in our business center, which is what we call the table with the coffeepot and the napkin-lined basket of doughnuts and assorted Danishes. She brought up the Web page for the Super Fun Castle in Tampa.

"It's their biggest and 'most funtastic' location," she said, reading the banner headline flashing on the screen.

"We need to see it," I said. "Figure out how to beat them."

Since we were still on vacation from school, Grandpa drove Gloria, me, and Dill (whose parents weren't really into the whole "Honey, let's entertain the kids" thing) to Tampa in his pickup truck to check out our new competition.

It was the Fun Castle mother ship.

They had dancing fountains, an actual castle, an indoor Mega Mini golf course, *and* an outdoor one, too! Their dinosaur, which was a thirty-foot-tall T. rex, roared and swung its tail across the putting green so you had to time your shot perfectly to put it into play—just like the windmill hole on our Stinky Beard course. That's right. They had a screeching, tail-thrashing, tiny-arm-wiggling T. rex. We had a windmill.

They also had a roller coaster.

"I'm not impressed," said Grandpa. "That dinosaur looks too new and shiny. How can it be prehistoric if it's shiny? And a roller coaster? This is Florida, not Coney Island!"

"Come on, let's go inside," suggested Gloria.

"Examine the full scope of their amusement offerings. Search for any weaknesses."

"That dinosaur looks pretty weak," said Grandpa. "See how tiny his arms are? Couldn't even pick up a bucket of chicken."

We passed another one of those Sir Laughsalot alligator guys working the parking lot.

"Here's a tip, son!" Grandpa said to the guy in the costume. "Alligators don't dance!"

"Except in that Walt Disney movie *Fantasia*," said Dill.

"Disney," hissed Grandpa. Then he started shaking his fist at the guy in the alligator suit. "Go back to Orlando, buddy! This is Tampa Bay! We don't like dancing alligators, talking ducks, *or* singing bears!"

A motion sensor made the Super Fun Castle's tinted glass doors magically whoosh open.

"Hey, ho, kiddos," chirped a cheery guy in khaki shorts and a polo shirt.

Well, he was cheery until his eyes adjusted to the blast of sunlight and he realized who we were.

I recognized him, too.

It was the funmeister we had just defeated on St. Pete Beach.

Bradley.

Who Wants to
Beat Bradley Badly?

"Oh," said Bradley, dropping his whole chipper-dipper act. "It's you. Defeat me once, shame on you. Defeat me twice, won't get defeated again."

"What?" said Gloria. "That makes absolutely no sense."

"I think what you meant to say—" Dill started, but Bradley cut him off.

"Doesn't matter. You motel maggots got lucky on St. Pete Beach. This round? You're going down!"

"You like to rhyme a lot, don't you?" I said.

Bradley grinned on one side of his face—the way dogs do right before they snarl. "What I like to do is win. That's why I put in for a transfer. This is my new B.O."

"You have B.O.?" said Grandpa. "In my day, we

didn't brag about such things. We used deodorant, too!"

"*B.O.* means 'base of operations,' old man! They bumped me up to head funmeister here at H.Q. And I've got all sorts of new ideas. *Winning* ideas."

Bradley glared at Grandpa hard. "I know how to beat you, old-timer. You wanna know why?"

"Not particularly . . ."

"Because I'm a professional winner. Winning isn't everything. It's the only thing. You? You're a dinosaur."

"And you're a bully!" I snapped.

"Aw. Are you going to melt, little snowflake?"

"P.T.'s not a snowflake," said Grandpa. "We don't have those in Florida. We have snowbirds."

I think Grandpa wanted to punch Bradley as much as I did, but Gloria suggested we all go home.

We didn't even check out their double Mega Mini golf courses.

Or the laser tag maze.

Or the flight simulator, even though that probably would've been fun. We could've practiced crashing and burning, which was what we were going to do in the regionals if we didn't totally up our game.

"Cheer up, kiddos," said Grandpa as we crossed the causeway to St. Pete Beach. "We'll swing by Laurette's office. See how our stocks are doing today. Maybe if we're up enough, we can cash out and use the money to build our own laser tag maze thingy inside a flight simulator."

"That would be neat, sir," said Dill. "Like being inside a *Star Wars* movie."

"Exactly! It'll go with my whole rocket ship

theme room. Now, I have a few friends at the airport. I'm guessing they have a spare flight simulator or two lying around. And lasers? Easy-peasy. We'll buy some of those red-dot pointers cats love. You put the two together, line the cockpit with glow-in-the-dark stars, and—*bing, bang, boom*—we've got a brand-new attraction: Lasers in Outer Space!"

We pulled into the strip mall on Gulf Boulevard where Ms. Oldewurtel had her offices.

The receptionist told us to take a seat and wait.

"Wait?" said Grandpa. He jokingly jutted out a thumb at Gloria. "This is Gloria Ortega. The wizard of Wall Street. The sage of St. Pete Beach."

That was when Ms. Oldewurtel came out of her office, looking frazzled.

"Is something wrong?" asked Gloria.

Ms. Oldewurtel nodded. "We need to talk."

"Have we peaked?"

"No, Gloria. We've tanked."

Not-So-Phantastic News

"It's my fault," said Gloria as we all climbed back into Grandpa's sweltering hot truck and crawled down Gulf Boulevard for home.

He believes in the old-fashioned kind of air-conditioning for cars—the kind where you crank open all the windows. It's like riding around in the dryer, except your clothes are all wet and sticking to your back.

"I wasn't watching CNBC like I should've been!" Gloria continued. "I wasn't tracking the minute-by-minute trades. I was too busy helping set up the Frolf tournament."

"Well, that was important, too," I said, sounding semi-defensive.

"And extremely fun," added Dill.

"What goes down must come back up!" said

Grandpa, trying to buck us up. "Unless there's a problem with the elevator. I had that happen once. Had to hike down twenty flights of stairs. . . ."

Gloria and Grandpa's stock portfolio wasn't completely wiped out. It was just worth about one tenth of what it had been three days earlier. That edible-eraser company was being sued by the parents of a kindergartner who had gagged on her chocolate-flavored kitty-cat pencil topper. The girl's father was a lawyer, the kind that does TV commercials about suing people when you slip on a grape at the grocery store.

No way were we building Grandpa's Lasers in Outer Space attraction anytime soon. And there would be no new theme rooms for the regional round, even though Grandpa had big ideas for a Jungle Room, complete with roaring cabinets, and one he called the Bermuda Triangle, where "your socks are guaranteed to get lost."

When we hit the motel, Grandpa headed off to his workshop to fix himself a bologna and mustard sandwich with extra pickles.

"Extra pickles always help me think better," he said.

Dill went to his room to check in with his parents.

Gloria and I stepped into the lobby and savored the sweet, sweet air-conditioned air. Seriously.

If it weren't for air-conditioning, everybody's clothes would turn into moist, mildewed towels—the soggy kind you find on the floor of a motel bathroom.

Mr. Ortega was at the front desk, showing Mom his phone.

"What's going on, Dad?" asked Gloria.

"Biff Billington just texted me a copy of what he claims will be his ESPN audition tape."

"He did a very cute interview with the Phillie Phanatic," said Mom.

Mr. Ortega winced a little.

"I'm sorry, Manny," said Mom, "but it's true. It's cute."

"I know," said Mr. Ortega, taking in a deep steadying breath. "Funny and heartwarming at the same time."

"Heartwarming?" said Gloria.

"The googly-eyed, funnel-nosed, green-feathered freak doesn't even talk!" I added.

"True," said Mr. Ortega. "But, oh, what a sad and woeful tale his silence can tell. Especially with weepy violins on the soundtrack."

Mr. Ortega showed us the video on his phone screen.

"Biff Billington is punking you," I said. "No way is that his real audition."

Mr. Ortega thought about that for a second. I

could tell he was thinking because he arched his left eyebrow.

"You might be right, P.T. Why else would he show me his hand?"

"He's trying to defeat you by getting you to do something equally ridiculous. Don't fall for it. Do like Gloria says: knit up your stockings!"

"Actually," said Gloria, "the expression is 'stick to your knitting.'"

"Sorry. My bad. But seriously, Mr. O, you should do that story with the teenaged golf prodigy. Johnny Zeng."

"He's definitely interested," said Mr. Ortega. "I was finally able to talk to his parents. They are quite protective of their son's privacy."

"Of course they are!" I said, snapping my fingers, because I was having one of my patented P. T. Wilkie brainstorms. "You see, more than anything, Johnny Zeng wants to be a regular sixteen-year-old kid. He wants to play video games, eat cheeseburgers, and go to the prom. Golf is his gift, but it's also his curse."

"Oooh," said Mr. Ortega. "I like this."

"I told you he was good at developing a back-story," said Gloria proudly.

It was time for my big finish, the most important part of any story, because that's all anybody's really interested in: what happens in the end?

"And what could be more 'regular kid' than playing a fun, frivolous, and surprisingly frustrating game known as Frolf?"

"Huh?" said Mr. Ortega, because I'd kind of lost him.

"Frolf! Frisbee golf. Shoot your boy wonder competing in the Wonderland Open Tournament."

"And when's that?"

"I'm not exactly sure. Whenever the judges decide to come back."

"Sunday," said Mom. "Sorry. Forgot to tell you guys. The magazine people called. They'll be back here in three and a half days."

You Gotta Have a Gimmick

Just like that, we had our gimmick.

That was a good thing, because we didn't have time or money to build a new attraction.

The Super Fun Castle might have had the technological edge and the cooler things for kids to do and a T. rex and a flight simulator and a laser tag maze and a roller coaster, but we were offering a once-in-a-lifetime opportunity: a chance to play Frolf with the one and only Johnny Zeng.

"We're gonna win Grandpa that trophy!" I said, ready for a "booyah" from Gloria.

Gloria didn't give me one.

"Slight problem," she said. We were hanging out in the front room of the suite where Mom and I live. The TV was on, but I'd muted the sound. Gloria and I had too much to plot and plan. We didn't need distractions. Unless a *Shark Tank* rerun came on. We love us some *Shark Tank*.

"Johnny Zeng could give us some very snackable content," said Gloria, "but right now, only Dad and some sports geeks at ESPN really know who this child prodigy with a putter is. Plus, we don't know what he looks like. Neither does Dad. There are zero images of him on the Internet. His parents have done an excellent job protecting his privacy."

"So we need to build him up," I told her. "Turn the mysterious Johnny Zeng into a star. They do it on TV all the time. Especially reality TV. What did the real housewives of wherever actually do to become TV stars? Nothing. They just had to be real. Sort of."

"We'll need an intensive social networking campaign. Twitter. Facebook. Instagram. Snapchat."

"Definitely."

Suddenly, something on the TV screen caught my eye.

A commercial for Tampa's Super Fun Castle. A spiraling starburst promised "Super Big News."

And there was Bradley, twirling a Frisbee on his index finger.

I grabbed the remote and pumped up the volume.

"Hey, ho, kiddos. Are you ready for some serious fun? Because the Super Fun Castle is proud to introduce the Tampa Bay area's first and only

Professional Disc Golf Association–approved Mega Mini Frolf course. And the pros from the PDGA already agree: it's the most challenging disc golf course in the Tampa Bay area. Everything else is just for amateurs and fly-by-night flingers."

Our new professional-grade Frolf course is dino-mite! Bring your girlfriend or boyfriend and enter the Flirtaceous era.

"So," said Bradley, wrapping up his spiel, "if you're looking for some serious fun in the sun, and not just some rinky-dink disc tossing around the grounds of an antique motel, storm the Super Fun Castle, home of Tampa Bay's top-rated PDGA Frolf course!"

Bradley had totally ripped us off and stolen our Frolf idea!

And then he'd done something worse.

He had made it better.

48

Beach Battle Plans

The Super Fun Castle wasn't our only competition. Snarlin' Garland's Alligator Alley, a go-kart racetrack in Sarasota, was the third finalist in the Tampa Bay regional competition.

My go-karts are so galdern fast y'all are gonna say, "Later, gator!"

?!

There would be no mystery shoppers this time. Those scores would carry over from the first round. The panel of judges would visit the Tampa branch of the Fun Castle chain on Friday, Snarlin' Garland's Alligator Alley on Saturday, and the Wonderland on Sunday.

Early Thursday morning—or, as I called it, T minus seventy-two hours—I gathered the troops (Mom, Gloria, Dill, and Grandpa) around the swimming pool and gave a little pep talk. Mr. Ortega was at his TV station, making final arrangements for Johnny Zeng's Sunday appearance at our Frolf course. Wheels were in motion! Now we just needed to get fired up for the coming beach battle.

"The Super Fun Castle may have Tampa Bay's newest, most impressive, and only PDGA-approved Frolf course," I said, marching back and forth with my hands clasped behind my back. (I'd seen a general do that in a movie once.) "But, ladies and gentlemen, we have something they never will. We have humor."

"Yes!" shouted Dill.

"We have heart."

"Hoo-ah!" shouted Dill.

"We have marvels to behold and stories to be told."

"Totally!" shouted Dill, whose family would be checking out after the weekend.

"P.T.?" said Grandpa. "I'm a little nervous. I saw a Super Fun Castle commercial on TV last night. There's this one hole where you have to toss your Frisbee around a helicopter crashing into a gas tanker that explodes just as your disc flies by."

"I'm thinking we can do the same thing!" said Grandpa. "I could pull out that old beat-up bumper car I have in my workshop and hook it up to the gas grill. When the flames start going, I toss a couple firecrackers and sparklers into the backseat . . ."

"We're not blowing anything up or setting anything on fire, Dad," said Mom, because she's practical that way.

"Well, we've got to do something spectacular!" cried Grandpa. "If we don't win the trophy this year, we may never have a chance to beat Disney again!"

"Technically," said Gloria, "Disney isn't in this competition."

"I know!" shouted Grandpa. "That's why we can beat him!"

Just then, Jimbo strolled around the corner from the parking lot. He was toting a couple of grocery sacks and was trailed by a mutt, a little dog that didn't look like any breed in particular.

The dog barked when it saw us. It was a very happy yap.

"Wow!" said Dill. "A dog!"

"Hey, guys," said Jimbo. "Hope you don't mind, but my little buddy Air Fur One heard you dudes might be flinging some more Frisbees around here today."

"Um, who, exactly, is Air Fur One?" I asked,

because somebody had to. (Gloria and Dill were too busy rubbing the rolled-over dog's belly.)

"He's a mutt I rescued from the shelter a couple weeks back," said Jimbo. "His name used to be Charlie. But last night, the neighbor's kids were out tossing a Frisbee around their backyard and, man, Charlie went bonkers. You should've seen him. Leaping up and twisting in the air. Reminded me of that basketball dude—you know, Air Jordan. That's when I knew I had to change his name, man. He isn't a Charlie. He's Air Fur One."

"He catches Frisbees?" I asked.

"Yuh-huh. He's a natural. Loves chasing those wobbly things so much, it's like he grew up eating kibble out of an upside-down disc!"

Air Fur One

"**W**e'll call Air Fur One our canine caddie," said Grandpa, throwing his arms open wide. "Jimbo? You're a genius! Come on. Get over here. You know I'm a hugger."

While Grandpa and Jimbo hugged it out (and Mom laughed), I grabbed a Frisbee out of the nearby laundry basket where we stored them between rounds of Frolf.

"Okay, bud," I said, "let's see what you've got."

I hurled the disc.

The dog flew after it.

I mean, he *flew*!

He chased the thing down, leapt off the ground, did a twisting spiral, snagged the Frisbee in his mouth, caught some major air, defied gravity for a few seconds, wafted back to earth, lightly touched down, and trotted back to proudly present me with his prize.

"Mom, can we keep him?" I said (because that's what kids are supposed to say whenever they fall in love with a dog).

"Yes," said Mom with a laugh.

"You can *borrow* him," said Jimbo. "He'll still be bunking with me."

"That dog is amazing!" said Grandpa. "He'll be bigger than P. T. Barnum's Jumbo!"

"Was Jumbo a dog?" asked Dill.

"No. An elephant. He was huge!"

"Yeah," I said. "I sort of got that from the name. . . ."

"Air Fur One will be heavily merchandisable," said Gloria. "I need to call a few suppliers."

She hurried up to her room.

"Jimbo," said Mom, smiling ear to ear, "why don't you grill our newest employee one of your special Surf Monkey burgers?"

"I think he might prefer my St. Pete sliders. More bite-size."

"Fine," said Mom. "And give him all he wants. It'll be his salary!"

● ● ●

For the rest of the day (with several breaks for shady naps, water bowl slurps, and mini-burger bites), Air Fur One entertained our guests with his incredible antics.

Nobody wanted to leave the Wonderland. Nobody was looking for something better to do. They wanted to play Frolf with the world's cutest and furriest caddie. It was amazing to watch the dog do the one thing he loved more than anything in the world: chase after a floating disc, acrobatically snag his target, and trot back triumphantly.

In the afternoon, Jimbo and I taught Air Fur One a new trick: dunking!

We trained the amazing disc-catching dog to snare a flying Frisbee as it neared the chain loops and flip it into the net below, giving several happy Frolf flingers an awesome assist.

Everybody—kids and grown-ups—wanted to have their picture taken with Air Fur One. Dill handled the digital camera and emailed official souvenir photos for a one-dollar service fee. Meanwhile, Gloria called her contacts and chased down adorable stuffed puppies and fluffy backpack danglers for her souvenir shop.

Mr. Ortega scored a firm commitment from Johnny Zeng's parents for the boy wonder to drop by the Wonderland on Sunday for a round of Frolf.

We launched a social media campaign, asking folks to help us pick the #MostFabulousFrolfer. Would it be #JohnnyZeng or #AirFurOne? We urged everybody to stop by @TheWonderland on Sunday for the #MightyFrolfBeachBattle.

Our posts were liked, loved, and retweeted like crazy. Buzz was building.

We had hope.

Sure, our attractions were sort of low-tech, but according to Gloria, they were also extremely high-touch, whatever that means.

Everything was going great.

Until nature called.

Beach Business

Air Fur One was playing the sand castle hole on the beach with a giggling family.

The dog dunked their disc into the net, touched down on the beach, and started circling the sand, sniffing the ground.

Guess he'd eaten too many of Jimbo's sliders.

He had to poop. Ahead of schedule.

And since he wasn't a cat, he forgot to bury his surprise in the sand.

"Duuuuude!"

Unfortunately, Air Fur One had decided to do his business right next to Corky's beach rental setup.

The laughing family who'd been Frolfing with our canine caddie scurried away from the scene of the crime.

"Don't worry!" I hollered as I trotted down to

Corky's stand. My first stop was a nearby trash barrel, where I did a quick search for a sheet of paper or a plastic bag—some kind of improvised pooper-scooper. I finally found something I could use: a red plastic cup.

"Whoa. What are you feeding that thing?" Corky asked as I shoveled up the dog's stinky deposit.

"Mostly sliders," I said.

"Switch to kibble, brah. And keep your gnarly little friend off my beach. He'll gross out my customers."

"Well," I said, trying to sound jolly, "don't forget—a lot of your customers are *our* customers."

"Yeah, about that," said Corky. "I've made an executive decision. No more discounts."

"Excuse me?"

"Business is booming, little brah. I don't need you or your guests anymore. Henceforth and forthwith, all discounts and courtesies previously extended to guests of the Wonderland Motel are hereby officially rescinded. In case you couldn't tell, I went to law school before I dropped out to study surfing. Chya!"

He did that thumb-and-pinkie *hang loose* thing surfers do.

"But we had a deal," I said.

"True. But now? We don't. Our deal expired, like, two minutes ago, right after your derelict doggy disrespected my business premises."

"Business premises? This is the beach."

"Which also happens to be my business address. I printed it on business cards and everything."

"B-b-but . . ."

"There he is!" shouted a familiar voice.

Mr. Frumpkes, whose mother lives a few doors down from our motel, marched as rapidly as anybody can when they try to hotfoot it across slippery sand in penny loafers. He was trailed by a police officer.

"That dog was on the beach!" Mr. Frumpkes told the cop. "That is strictly against all posted ordinances. That mutt is a menace!"

Dogs are the most disgusting creatures on the planet!

You ever looked in a mirror, pal?

In the Doghouse

The police officer—a guy named Josh David, who'd been a pal of Grandpa's for years (they go out for root beer floats and big chewy pretzels together sometimes)—was very nice.

"You know, P.T.," he said when Mr. Frumpkes was done screaming, "Fort De Soto and Honeymoon Island both have some awesome dog beaches."

"Fantastic," snarled Mr. Frumpkes. "Maybe you and your annoying family can move there, Mr. Wilkie. Just be sure to take your filthy sand pooper with you."

"There's no need for the Wilkies to move," said Officer David.

"Whatever," said Corky. "Just keep your kooky dog and floppy discs off the beach."

"Or next time," said Mr. Frumpkes, "you'll both end up in the dog pound!"

"No, they won't," said Officer David.

"They should!" insisted Frumpkes.

"Not really. We don't put kids in the dog pound, Mr. Frumpkes. You're a teacher. You should know that."

"Don't you tell me what I should know, Joshua. It's not too late to hold you back in seventh grade!"

"Yes, it is."

While they argued, Air Fur One grumbled a low rumbly growl.

Me too.

We both liked Officer David. But neither of us was too keen on Corky *or* Mr. Frumpkes. They weren't what you might call man's, or dog's, best friends.

But as nice as Officer David was, he had to lay down the law.

"All Frolf activities must be confined to the Wonderland's actual property," he told me as I cradled Air Fur One in my arms so that, technically, he wasn't *on* the beach.

"But the sand castle hole is one of our best," I explained. "Everyone loves riding the zip line down to it."

"Yeah," said Officer David. "You guys have got to cut that out, too."

"No more zip line?"

"Remove the pole, P.T. Today. If, you know, that works for you guys."

"Yes, sir."

"I can lend you a hand."

"Thanks."

While Mr. Frumpkes and Corky stood there watching us, Officer David and I wrested the steel pole out of the ground. Well, actually, Officer David did most of the pole wiggling. I was still holding Air Fur One.

"You anchored it with concrete?" he asked when he saw the gravel-heavy, bucket-shaped evidence at the bottom of the pole.

"Yeah."

"Don't do that again."

"Right."

Supersized Fun

Friday, Grandpa took Gloria, Dill, and me back to the Super Fun Castle in Tampa to see what kind of show they put on for the judges.

As we pulled into the ginormous parking lot, all sorts of super-eager kids in khakis and polo shirts wiggle-waggled orange-cone flashlights to direct us to our parking spot.

We ended up in the Lord Snicker Whoop area. There was a metal sign with the jolly knight's face on it. He looked extremely happy and only slightly dented.

The parking lot's enormous video billboard was blasting a looping movie showing slow-motion excitement on the "only PDGA-approved Frolf course in the Tampa Bay area."

The clips of course included the crashing helicopter (you had to fling your disc through its slowly rotating blades before the gas tanker blew up), the animatronic T. rex snatching Frisbees out of the air with its tiny arms, and some kind of virtual reality hole where you went up against a flock of ninjas throwing spinning-star discs.

"Very impressive," said Gloria.

"Sure," said Grandpa. "If you like loud noises, crashing helicopters, angry dinosaurs, and too much smoke. Smoking is bad for you. The health department should close this place down. You kids go ahead. I've seen enough. If this is what passes for fun in the sun these days, then I want to move to the North Pole!"

Grandpa ambled back to his truck.

My heart sank as I watched him walk away.

It seemed to me that for probably the first time in his life, Grandpa was giving up on his dreams.

Pros, Not Poetry

Gloria, Dill, and I trudged across the parking lot.

"Hey, ho, kiddos!"

It was that snap-happy alligator mascot, Sir Laughsalot.

"Welcome to the Super Fun Castle, where you're going to have a super-fun time or my name isn't Sir Laughsalot!"

"It isn't," I said. "That's a costume. Your real name is probably Luke. Or Ryan. Maybe Zachary."

"Wowzers," the cheery mascot said, chuckling. "Some grumpy Gus sure needs an attitude adjustment! No problem! Just step inside my super-fun castle for some supersized fun!"

"Yeah, right. Whatever."

We slumped toward the entrance. Except for Dill. The kid had a real spring in his step. Probably because it wasn't his family's motel that was about to be humiliated by the big boys in Tampa.

We made our way through what seemed like a five-acre-wide video arcade and past the weirdly iridescent glow-in-the-dark Mega Mini indoor golf course.

"Hey, look at my teeth!" said Dill. "You could even say they glow. You guys want to play a quick game of bucket toss?"

"No thanks," I said.

"How about Skee-Ball?"

Gloria and I both shook our heads.

"So I guess bowling is out of the question?"

"We're not really here to have fun, Dill," I said as gently as I could.

"Then what's the point?"

"Research," said Gloria. "Market analysis. Competitive decisioning."

"We need to see how they try to wow the judges," I said. "So we can out-wow 'em!"

We finally made it to the grandstands that had been set up around the outdoor Mega Mini course so that spectators could watch the night's main event, the Super Jackpot Flingarama. It was billed as an Ultimate Frolf round featuring the top pros in the game. All of them were champions of the PDGA. Fortunately, none of them would be Johnny Zeng. We still had that ace up our sleeve, which I think is an expression that means you're going to cheat at cards.

We didn't want to cheat.

We just wanted to win.

I saw Ms. Matchy-Matchy and the other judges sitting on a special riser set up under a bright blue awning. They were all sipping soft drinks out of souvenir cups molded to look like medieval knights and chowing down on sugar-dusted funnel cakes. They looked like they were having a great time.

"Ladies and gentlemen, boys and girls," boomed the kind of voice you usually hear only at NASCAR events or the circus, "it's time for our pros to tee off. Or, as we say here at the Super Fun Castle, it's blastoff time!"

That was when about a bajillion fireworks lit up the sky in sync to a song called "Disco Inferno." I guess because it was "disc" golf.

And then the four pros took the field.

The guy in the middle?

Our old friend Bradley.

Racing to the Bottom

It was a very long, very quiet ride home.

When we reached the Gandy Bridge, the three-mile-long concrete span connecting Tampa and St. Petersburg, Dill finally spoke up.

"Wow. They sure are serious about their Frolf at the Super Fun Castle."

"Yep," I said. "They sure are."

"That Bradley is such a meanie," said Dill. "The lady Frolfer falling into the gator pit on the fourth hole wasn't an accident. Bradley tripped her."

"Yeah," I said. "I saw that, too. Good thing the alligators weren't real."

"They weren't?" said Dill. "That's a relief."

"They're audio-animatronic," I explained. "Like the ones on the jungle boat ride over at Disney World."

Grandpa gripped the steering wheel a little harder.

"Disney World," he said through clenched teeth.

He probably would've shaken his fist at the heavens and said something else, but there were kids riding in the truck with him.

I knew how he felt.

Disney. Grandpa's longtime rival. His nemesis. His personal Darth Vader (who, by the way, Disney now owns). Disney wasn't in this competition, but now we were up against the pyrotechnics at the Super Fun Castle plus the all-out, nonstop go-kart action at Snarlin' Garland's Alligator Alley.

In case you've never heard of him, Snarlin' Garland Dupree is a former hot-rodder and demolition derby superstar who grew up near the Everglades. A true Florida "gator," he crushed the competition in monster truck rallies all across the country in a souped-up vehicle he called the Chomper. It was shaped like an alligator, with hydraulic snapping jaws up front. That was how he *crushed* the competition. Literally.

At his go-kart track, all the cars are shaped like alligators.

We went up to Snarlin' Garland's on Saturday morning so we could check out the road rally they'd be staging for the panel of judges.

Mom drove us this time.

Once again, slick professional greeters helped us park our car and find our seats.

The Snarlin' Garland's experience, I have to admit, was pretty awesome. Roaring engines. Snazzy alligator cars. Cool helmets and jumpsuits with gas station and oil company patches plastered all over them.

The racetrack had an awesome Everglades theme. You had to race around swamps and panthers and pythons and ten-foot-tall mutant mosquitoes.

Video clips of Snarlin' Garland shouting "Shoo-wee!" and "Dadgum, that's good gas-pedalin'!" and "Go get 'er, gators!" played on a JumboTron score-board between races.

We all took a spin around the track in our mini-gator go-karts. It was awesome.

When we crossed the finish line and climbed out of our rides, one of the cool pit crew bosses—a college girl in make-believe mechanic overalls—ran over to us.

"Hey there, gang!" she said. "We need one more racer for the Hot Gator Five Hundred!"

"One of *us*?" said Dill.

"Yep!"

Dill started hopping up and down.

He seemed excited. More excited than usual.

The Thrill of the Dill

"What's the Hot Gator Five Hundred?" asked Dill eagerly.

"It's a five-lap race around the track and today's main event," said the pit crew boss. "The winner will be going home with five hundred Atomic Fireballs!"

Dill's eyes nearly popped out of his skull. "Those red-hot cinnamon jawbreakers?"

"That's right!"

"I *love* Atomic Fireballs!"

"Well, then, climb back into your gator kart. You have another race comin' up!"

Dill turned to Gloria and me. He had a sheepish look on his face.

"Does either of you guys want to race in the Hot Gator Five Hundred instead?"

"Nope," I said. "The Atomic Fireballs are all yours."

"As much as I enjoyed our spin around the track," said Gloria, "I'm not a major go-kart fan. Even ones molded to resemble crocodilian reptiles. I'm also not very keen on Atomic Fireballs. They turn my tongue red."

"Exactly!" said Dill.

I clapped him on the shoulder and said, "Go win the big race, Dill. Just promise us one thing."

"Sure. Anything. What is it?"

"That you'll have fun."

"Definitely!"

The pit crew boss showed Dill where the starting line for the big race would be. Gloria and I made our way up to the bleachers, where we'd watch the main event with Mom, who had already ordered us a big box of cheesy nachos.

(You ever wonder how they get that pumpable nacho cheese to be so orange and gloppy? Me too. But I don't think I want to know.)

The Hot Gator 500 race was incredible.

We could hear Dill's giggles and shrieks all the way up in the fifteenth row. They were louder than the screaming engines and the screeching tires combined.

When the checkered flag fell, Dill was in the lead. He crossed the finish line first and zoomed into the winner's circle, where the pit crew boss presented him with a loving cup trophy overflowing with Atomic Fireballs.

My breath will smell like cinnamon mouthwash forever!

As happy as I was that Dill had won, I realized that the Wonderland had sort of lost.

Because I could see the panel of judges giving Dill and Snarlin' Garland's Alligator Alley racetrack a standing ovation.

Snarlin' with Garland

Dill waved to us to come down and join him and Snarlin' Garland in the winner's circle.

"You guys?" said Dill. "This is Snarlin' Garland Dupree! The real deal!"

The big man shot out his hand.

"How y'all doin'?" he asked. "Dill here tells me you folks are related to the one and only Walt Wilkie!"

"He's my father," said Mom.

I smiled proudly. "And my grandpa."

"He's sort of my grandpa, too," said Gloria. "I guess. Kind of."

"Totally," I said. "You guys are definitely like family."

"I just met him," said Dill. "But he's awesome."

"That he is, little man," said Snarlin' Garland,

rubbing Dill's bristly crew cut. "You folks enjoy the race?"

"We certainly did," said Mom.

Garland laughed. "It were galdern fun, weren't it?"

"Yes," said Mom, "it were."

"Well, ma'ams, sirs, that's what Alligator Alley is all about. Sizzlin', smokin', tailpipe-chokin', goin'-for-broke'in fun in the sun. You know where I got the idea to turn go-karts into alley-gators?"

"The zoo?" suggested Dill.

"Nope. From an old-school attraction I used to frequent when I was your all's age." He pointed at Dill, Gloria, and me. Not Mom. "Place called Walt Wilkie's Wonder World."

Mom smiled. "Is that so?"

"Yes, ma'am. I tell you what, your diddy and granddiddy? Back in the day, that man was a world-class entertainer and impresario. He used to have this merry-go-round with all sorts of silly saddled critters. Ducks, geese, turtles, bunny rabbits, and one big, honkin' gator. That's the one I always wanted. 'Gotta git us the gator,' I'd tell my diddy. We'd go runnin', beat everybody else. They all wanted that gator. See, I remembertated that when I built this here go-kart track.

"Good times," he said. "Walt Wilkie knew how to make anything fun. Even a liddy-biddy railroad

looping around his parking lot. I still have a ton of tin stars I earned being deputized on that particular ride for fightin' off the train robbers. It was galdern fun 'cause that, ladies and gents, was always the Walt Wilkie way."

"Um, maybe you haven't heard," I said, "but he's up against you in this competition."

"Is that so? I didn't see Wonder World on the list."

"We're called the Wonderland now," said Mom. "We're a motel."

"And semi–amusement park," I added. "We have attractions. Shows."

"Well, dang," said Garland, "I sure hope y'all win."

"Huh?" I said.

"Shoot, son. Your granddiddy practically invented Florida-style fun in the sun. About time somebody gave *him* a galdern tin star or trophy for it."

More Daydreams

Mom drove us home to the Wonderland around noon.

We were all feeling pretty good after hearing Snarlin' Garland rave about Grandpa. All of us also had scorched tongues, because Dill insisted on sharing his Atomic Fireballs.

"I still have like four hundred and ninety left!" he said as we pulled into the parking lot.

Through the lobby windows, we could see Mr. Ortega doing his end zone dance again. It reminded me of a flamingo walking across a waffle iron.

"Wonder what he's so happy about," Mom said as we all climbed out of the car.

"Maybe he heard about my go-kart race!" said Dill. "He probably wants to put me on the WTSP sports report! I better take these to my room before they melt."

Dill ran off with his jawbreakers. The rest of us trooped into the lobby and learned the real reason for Mr. Ortega's happy dance.

"ESPN loves my Johnny Zeng angle!" he said with a sideways arm pump. "They just texted me. Ladies and gentlemen, put thirty seconds on the shot clock. It's do-or-die time. Johnny Z will land tomorrow at two p.m. After we chitchat, we'll shoot some B-roll of his first foray into Frolf."

I didn't think I'd ever seen Mr. O so pumped.

"Congratulations, Dad," said Gloria.

"ESPN loved the child-prodigy-gets-to-be-a-normal-kid angle. So kudos to you on that, P.T."

"Glad I could help."

Mr. Ortega struck a pose and checked his reflection in the mini mirror at the top of our sunglasses rack.

"Yes, sports fans, the chair behind the ESPN desk is still wide open. It's anybody's game. Sure, Biff Billington has some quality wins on his demo reel, but I think I'm peaking at just the right time!"

"That's such great news, Manny," said Mom.

She was smiling, but I could tell it was the kind of smile that sort of hurts. She was happy for Mr. Ortega. But I think she was sad for herself.

ESPN's studios are in Bristol, Connecticut, not St. Petersburg, Florida. If Mr. Ortega became one of the big dogs at ESPN, he'd be moving out of the Wonderland. Heck, he'd be moving out of the state.

Also, if Mr. Ortega moved to Connecticut, chances were he'd take his daughter.

I wasn't sure how *I'd* handle that.

Gloria and I had become a pretty awesome team. She was the steak; I was the sizzle. I had the wacky ideas; she knew how to make them work. She was also an extremely excellent friend.

I probably would've said something silly to cheer Mom up (it's what I usually do), but I heard a scream and a *kerthud* out back.

"Aw, nuts!"

It was Grandpa.

Brontosaurus Wrecks

Grandpa had been very, very busy while we were in Sarasota checking out Snarlin' Garland's Alligator Alley.

He'd sawed the tail off Dino, our giant fiberglass dinosaur statue, and tried to reattach it with the kind of knuckle hinges you'd use on a shed door.

"I'm trying to get it to swish and sway," he explained when we all ran out to see what had caused the crash. He was tightening up some screws on the wing plates connecting the sawed-off tail to the dinosaur's (now) stubby butt. Dill was there, watching him.

"If it works," said Grandpa, "it'll be just like that T. rex hazard at the Super Fun Castle."

He uncoiled a yellow nylon rope he'd looped

around the tip of Dino's tail, and raced to the far side of the parking lot.

"The Super Fun Castle's got nothing on us!" he hollered. "Watch this!"

Grandpa gave the line a good, strong yank.

The dinosaur tail popped off and crashed to the pavement. Again.

"Aw, nuts! It was supposed to wag!"

"Dad?" said Mom.

"Yes, Wanda?"

She sighed. A real shoulder-sagger. "Never mind."

She went back to the lobby. Mr. Ortega went with her. Because, like I said before, he's a good guy.

"Your thinking is sound, Mr. Wilkie," Gloria said to Grandpa. "Animating the statue would definitely put us on a more equal footing with our primary competitor."

"Or," said Dill, trying to be helpful, "you could load the tail with my Atomic Fireballs, and it could be like a prehistoric piñata. Every time you yanked off the tail, candy would pour out."

Grandpa dropped the rope.

"Ah, who am I trying to kid?" said Grandpa. It sounded as if somebody had knocked all the air out of him. All the spirit and fight, too.

"I'm no Walt Disney. Never have been. Never will be."

"You don't have to be!" I told him. "You're Walt *Wilkie*!"

He nodded. "Right. The one that nobody's ever heard of."

"Snarlin' Garland has," I told him.

"Is that so?"

"He thinks you're awesome," added Dill.

"Nope. I'm just a nobody who's never done much of anything."

"Don't say that, Grandpa," I begged. "Come on. It's like I read in a book once. The game isn't really over until it's over."

"This game is done, P.T. Finished. Kaput. As Gloria's father says all the time on TV, the fat lady has sung."

"That," Gloria explained to Dill, "is an unfortunate and somewhat stereotypical sportscaster reference to opera, many of which end with a lady of some heft and girth singing—usually in a winged helmet."

"Oh," said Dill. "I did not know that."

Grandpa wasn't listening to any of us. He flapped his hand at the world.

"We should've sold out to Mr. Conch and moved to Arizona like your mother wanted to," he said. "I'm too old to be acting like a big kid."

"I find your antics to be quite amusing, sir," said Dill.

"Well, Dill, to tell you the truth, right now I just find them to be sad. And exhausting. Oy. I need a bologna sandwich. And a nap."

He hobbled off to his workshop. It was like he had aged fifteen years in fifteen seconds.

We all probably should've been getting ready for our big Sunday with the judges. We barely had twenty-four hours to prepare for their arrival.

But nobody was in the mood. Sure, we still had the Frolf tournament and Johnny Zeng, but compared to all the action at the Super Fun Castle and the Hot Gator 500, they seemed pretty puny.

Gloria went up to her room to plot her stock portfolio picks for when the market reopened on Monday. "We still have a little money in our account. I might be able to orchestrate a rally."

Dill went back to his room, too.

Me?

I sank to the curb and started thinking about what a horrible mistake I'd made.

I had wanted to make Grandpa's lifelong dream come true.

I had wanted him to see himself in the same league as Walt Disney, because that was where I'd seen him my whole life. To me, Grandpa was way bigger than Disney.

He had given me everything.

But I couldn't give him the one thing he wanted more than anything in the world.

I felt like a dinosaur with a tail that wouldn't wag.

Useless.

Doggedly Determined

While I was sitting there moping, feeling sorry for myself, Air Fur One trotted over.

He was carrying a plastic disc in his mouth, but he dropped it at my feet so he could hop up, put his front paws on my knees, and lick my face.

I don't speak Dog. But I think his wet tongue was trying to tell me, *Snap out of it, pal!*

"Okay," I said, "you want to play?"

I bent down and picked up the Frisbee.

His tail wag told me, *You bet!*

I flung the disc.

It floated toward the pool.

He leapt up, snared the wobbly plastic plate, and gently touched down. Then he trotted back with the Frisbee, which he once again dropped at my feet.

I picked it up and gave it another fling.
He chased it down and brought it back.
I tossed, he retrieved.

We kept at it for maybe half an hour.

No matter where I hurled that disc, no matter what obstacles he had to overcome, the dog went after it. He just wouldn't quit, maybe because he loved what he was doing so much.

Maybe because he knew how good he was at it.

Air Fur One definitely had a talent.

And so did I.

I had a wild imagination and a real knack for making up stories. So maybe that was all we really needed to win the *Florida Fun in the Sun* competition. Maybe Grandpa had forgotten what he'd taught me years ago, but I hadn't: "Sell the sizzle, P.T., not the steak."

"Come here, boy!" I shouted.

Air Fur One finally dropped the disc and leapt up into my arms.

"I get it!" I told him. "I won't give up, either. No matter what."

And while the dog licked my face like I was an all-day meat loaf sucker, Jimbo ambled over, wiping his hands on a dishrag he uses to mop up the counter at the Banana Shack.

"Looks like Air Fur One did the job I sent him over here to do."

"Yeah," I said. "He sure did."

"Well, guess what, man? It's time for you to go do yours!"

Running with the Big Dogs

It was about two o'clock on Saturday.

The judges would be dropping by the Wonderland at two o'clock on Sunday. That meant we had a whole day to clutch victory from the jaws of defeat, which is something Mr. Ortega said one time when he was reporting on a high school football game. It figures that defeat has jaws. Well, I wasn't going to be gulped down without a fight.

I called a quick meeting of the Wonderland Motel Brain Trust. That's basically Gloria. I also invited Dill, because the kid seemed to get a kick out of hanging with us.

"You guys," I said when we were assembled around a table at the Banana Shack, "we can still win this thing. We have the golf wunderkind Johnny Zeng. We have Air Fur One. We have the banana cream pie, mermaid, bologna sandwich, and game rooms. So, what do those other guys have that we don't?"

"Exploding helicopters," said Dill. "And kick-butt go-karts."

"I mean besides the physical stuff, the stuff we can't build in less than a day."

"Well," said Gloria, "if I may?"

She opened up a small spiral notebook, where I guessed she'd been jotting down her competitive analysis homework.

"The customer service personnel at both Snarlin' Garland's Alligator Alley and the Super Fun Castle have a much more polished and professional appearance than we maintain here."

She was looking at me when she said that. I probably hadn't tucked my shirt into my pants since the last time Mom and I had gone to the Don CeSar Hotel for Mother's Day brunch.

"They wear a lot of polo shirts," said Dill. "And the shirts are all the same color."

"Their pants are uniformly khaki," added Gloria.

"Oh, and they have name tags!" said Dill.

"Okay," I said, "we can do all that. You guys have polo shirts and tan shorts, right? Plus, Jack Alberto has a label maker. He can print out name badges for everybody on the staff."

"Can I be on the staff?" asked Dill.

"Definitely. In fact, I have an idea." I turned to Gloria. "I don't know if this is in your notes . . ."

"It probably is."

"But both the Super Fun Castle and Snarlin' Garland's have costumed mascots. Sir Laughsalot and the pit crew kids."

Gloria tapped the page in her notebook. "My third bullet point. Right after parking attendants with orange airport-cone flashlights."

"We need a mascot," I said.

"Ooh, ooh," said Dill, raising his hand. "I could be a mascot. I saw some Halloween costumes across the street in that store where we got the water gun gear!"

"I saw those, too," I said. "One of them was a dog, which would be perfect. You could be Air Fur One's big brother—Air Fur Too."

Wow! I have a sudden urge to chase my own tail!

AIR FUR TOO

"And," said Dill, "I could carry Frisbees around in my mouth."

Gloria shook her head. "Bad and semi-unsanitary idea. Just meet and greet."

"I'll write you up some stuff to say," I told Dill. "Because that's another thing I noticed about our competition—they're both very tightly scripted."

Gloria nodded. "Bullet point number seven. They also have video screens in the parking lots to promote their major attractions."

"We can do that," I said. "We have a ton of TVs. We can roll one out of an empty room and park it underneath the Welcome to Wonderland sign out front. I'll create some kind of splashy graphics on the computer, transfer the file to your laptop . . ."

"Which," said Gloria, "I'll link to the TV with an HDMI cable."

"Booyah!"

We did a three-way knuckle knock.

And then we went to work.

Because we only had twenty-three hours and thirty minutes to make the Wonderland as slick and polished as we could.

Polishing Our Act

I don't think I've ever worked harder at anything in my life.

We put together sharp-looking uniforms—once we realized that just about everybody owns a navy-blue polo shirt and a pair of khaki shorts.

Jack Alberto came over with his label maker. In a flash, we all had semiofficial–looking name tags. Jack and his younger brother, Nate, volunteered to be our parking lot attendants. We gave them light-up jack-o'-lantern flashlights left over from Hallow-een. (It was the closest thing I could find in our storage shed to official airport-cone lights.)

Clara, our head housekeeper, and the rest of the staff went around polishing and buffing every-thing that needed spiffing up, including the statues. They shined our Morty D. Mouse statue until it was so bright that you could see your reflection in his cheese wedge. They used Windex on the windows to the Banana Cream Pie Room (which was currently vacant) on the first floor so Frolfers could look in and ooh and aah at it while they waited to tee off.

Dill dashed across the street to Shore Enuff Stuff and bought his Air Fur Too costume.

Mom, who'd found her own navy-blue polo shirt, was tidying up the lobby and restocking the soft drink machines. She took out Grandpa's Cel-Ray cans and put them in our kitchen fridge. "It's an acquired taste," she said. "And so far, Dad is the only one I know who's acquired it."

Mr. Ortega was up in his room, making sure everything was "locked down tight" for Johnny Zeng's big arrival.

Everybody was pumped.

Even Grandpa.

When he saw all of us bustling around the property, he came out of his workshop and his funk.

"P.T.?" he said. "What the heck is going on? What's with the spit-and-polish job? Why are you wearing those clothes? You look like an insurance salesman on his day off."

"Well, Grandpa," I told him, "we're not giving up without a fight!"

"You shouldn't, either, sir," said Gloria.

"I agree," said Dill, flopping down his hands at the wrists so they resembled paws. Then he panted. I had to hand it to him: the kid did a good dog.

"Okay, okay, okay," said Grandpa. "I get the picture. Now, if you'll excuse me, I need to put a fresh mustard-scented candle in the Bologna on White Bread Room!"

Frolf Time!

Sunday dawned and we were as ready as we could be.

Mr. Ortega had plugged Johnny Zeng's two o'clock appearance at the Wonderland Motel on his sportscast the night before.

Our parking lot was packed.

Air Fur One was prancing around, wagging his tail, greeting guests. Dill was out there doing the same—in costume.

"Welcome to the Wonderland!" he said, reciting the script we had worked up together. "I'm doggone glad to see you! I'm sure you'll have a pawsome time!"

Jack and Nate were waving their orange pumpkin flashlights, directing cars. Our new "video sign" was filled with a slow-motion montage of Air Fur

One's airborne antics set to techno music blasting out of a boom box.

Gloria and her Junior Achievement gang were running the souvenir table, selling a ton of stuffed dogs, commemorative flying discs, and dog-shaped sugar cookies. Out back at the Banana Shack, Jimbo

was grilling special Air Fur One hot dogs, in honor of the "hottest dog" on the Frolf circuit.

Grandpa was strolling around in his silly golf pants and floppy hat.

It was awesome!

A little before two, Johnny Zeng arrived with a young woman in a business suit. Johnny was a gangly sixteen-year-old guy wearing golfing gloves, spiked shoes, and a baseball cap.

"Johnny Zeng, I presume?" cried Mr. Ortega, jutting out his hand to shake the golfer's. "Welcome! Thanks for agreeing to do your first-ever interview with yours truly. Who'd you bring with you today?"

"Heather," said Zeng.

"I'm his agent," said the lady in the suit.

"Well, welcome."

Mr. Ortega's camera crew turned on their blazing lights, raised the boom microphone, and went to work.

"So, Johnny," said Mr. Ortega, beaming his smile, "welcome to the world-famous Wonderland Motel here on St. Pete Beach in Florida."

"This place is famous?" said Johnny, looking around and making a stinky face. "For what? Being boring?"

Mr. Ortega did his professional-sports-reporter chuckle. "Heh-heh-heh. For being in a movie. But enough about the motel. Are you ready to catch disc-flinging fever?"

Johnny shrugged. "I guess."

"Then hey, hey, Tampa Bay—let's get to it."

"In a minute."

"Huh?"

"Johnny needs to wait," said his agent. "For his coach."

"Your golf coach?" asked Mr. Ortega.

"No," said Johnny. "New guy."

Mr. Ortega looked a little stunned, so I jumped right in.

"Um, any idea when your new coach will be here?"

"Soon."

Johnny Zeng was a teen of few words. I guess a lot of them are.

So we waited.

Until a guy on a thrumming motorcycle pulled into the parking lot, totally ignoring Jack and Nate and their pumpkin flashlights.

The biker parked where he felt like parking and whipped off his helmet.

It was Bradley. From the Super Fun Castle.

Coach Bradley

"Hiya, Johnny," said Bradley.

"Hey, Bradley."

"*You're* his coach?" I asked as Bradley climbed off his Harley.

"You bet."

He undid the bungee cords tying down his gym bag to the back of the bike.

"I reached out to Johnny and his people late last night after I caught the sports report on WTSP. Manny said he'd be here at two o'clock for the first-ever on-camera interview with Johnny Z."

"That I did," said Mr. Ortega, proudly bouncing up on the balls of his feet.

"Big fan, sir," said Bradley, holding out his hand.

Mr. Ortega shook it. "Thanks for watching. At WTSP, we put the T.S.P. in Tampa, St. Pete."

"Huh?"

"Wait a second," I said to Bradley. "You called Johnny Zeng at, like, eleven-thirty? Last night?"

Bradley smiled smugly. "He who hesitates is lost—which, by the way, makes him a loser."

"And as his coach, will you be Frolfing with him? Today?"

"I prefer to call it disc golfing."

"Fine," I said. "We'll just raffle off *two* spots in Johnny Zeng's foursome instead of three."

Now Bradley was shaking his head. "Not going to happen, kid. It's just going to be me and Johnny Z."

"B-b-but . . ."

"If you have a problem with that, we can deep-six this interview and I'll take Johnny over to the Super Fun Castle, where he can see what it's like to play on a professional-grade course."

"Ooh," said Johnny's agent. "That sounds amazing."

Mr. Ortega's eyes widened. This interview was supposed to be his big break, his ticket to ESPN.

I couldn't let Bradley crush his dreams.

"Fine," I said, handing Johnny and Bradley two official Wonderland Frisbees from a laundry basket.

"No thanks," said Bradley, unzipping his gym bag. "We brought our own." He pulled out two jet-black discs. "They're professional grade. Just like me and Johnny."

"Well, hey, hey, Tampa Bay," said Mr. Ortega,

rolling into his TV catchphrase. Again. "Let's get to it."

Johnny Zeng, his agent, Bradley, Mr. Ortega, and the camera crew marched over to the first tee box with their shiny, aerodynamically perfect black discs.

And of course, as soon as Bradley and Johnny Zeng were ready to fling off, the judges arrived.

Here Come the Judges

The panel of five judges who would determine the Wonderland's fate cruised into the parking lot in a big van wrapped with a vinyl *Florida Fun in the Sun* decal.

"Places, everybody!" shouted Grandpa. "It's showtime!"

The van door slid open, and out climbed the lady we'd labeled Ms. Matchy-Matchy and her son, Geoffrey. I recognized the other judges from our visits to the regional rounds at the Super Fun Castle and Alligator Alley.

"Welcome to the Wonderland, ladies and gentlemen," I said. "We hope you have a wonderful, funderful time!"

Dill bopped over in his dog costume. "Pardon my inter-ruff-tion, everybody, but I hope you folks have a pawsitively pawsome time!"

Geoffrey giggled.

I started my welcome speech.

"This, of course, ladies and gentlemen, is the world-famous Wonderland Motel. I'm P. T. Wilkie. Before I worked here, I worked at an orange juice factory. But my boss had to fire me. I couldn't concentrate."

As you know, we don't allow line cutting here at the world-famous Wonderland. Anyone caught with a pair of scissors will be asked to leave.

"My," said Ms. Matchy-Matchy when I finished my welcome spiel. "I love how you spiffed the place up since our last visit. And the snappy dialogue? Clever. Very clever. Are those new uniforms?"

"Yes, ma'am," I said proudly, patting down my name tag label, because it was sort of curling up and peeling off my shirt. "And wait till you meet the newest member of our fun-in-the-sun team: Air Fur One! The disc-catching dog!"

"There's a dog?" squealed Geoffrey.

"Two!" said Dill, doing his paws-up/panting act again.

"I want to meet the real dog, not you!" said Geoffrey.

"Well," I said, doing my best to sound like the tour guides on the jungle boat ride at Disney World, "you'll find him around back, sitting in the shade, because Air Fur One sure doesn't want to turn into a hot dog."

Geoffrey did a quick goody-goody, jumpy-clappy thing and took off for the Banana Shack.

His mother grinned. "Excellent display of hospitality," she said, tapping her temple. "I'm making a mental note. Oh, I see that fellow from the Super Fun Castle is here. . . ."

She'd seen Bradley.

"Yes, ma'am."

She put her hand alongside her mouth and whispered, "That must mean your Frolf course is more fun-in-the-sun than his!"

I breathed a sigh of relief.

We were golden.

We were going to win Grandpa his prize!

Or so I thought.

Until I heard what sounded like an earthquake.

65

Giant Disaster

The thundering crash came from the Banana Cream Pie Room.

Grandpa was on the landing outside, panicking.

"The whipped-cream ceiling just flattened the pie-tin bed!" he hollered. "Good thing nobody was in the room!"

Mom and Gloria ran over to see what all the commotion was about. Plaster dust billowed out from under the door. Tourists were gasping. So were the judges. Bradley was the only one in the whole crowd smiling. In fact, he was sniggering—which is like laughing, only meaner.

Our first-floor theme room didn't look like a delicious dessert anymore.

It looked like a disaster zone.

"Oh, my," said Ms. Matchy-Matchy, standing right behind me.

I figured she was making another one of those mental notes.

"Was that supposed to happen?" she asked.

I looked to Grandpa. He stood there, frozen, his eyes wide with panic.

I looked at Mom. She nodded, letting me know I should do whatever I thought I needed to do—no matter how preposterous.

So I did what I do best. I spun a story. A real whopper.

"Yes, ladies and gentlemen, boys and girls," I told the assembled crowd, "this is what happens when a giant gets tired of sleeping in the clouds and checks into your motel."

I gestured to the room on the second floor directly above the remains of the Banana Cream Pie Room.

"The guy has huge shoes. Boots the size of boats. Guess he must've kicked them off."

"There's a giant up in that room?" asked Geoffrey.

"Yep," I said. "The Super Fun Castle may have crashing helicopters, but we have crashing ceilings."

"It looks like somebody had a *giant* pie fight in there!" said someone close to the window.

"Good one, sir," I said. Everyone laughed. "According to his driver's license, this giant hails from San Francisco. I think he plays baseball."

More laughter.

Grandpa shot me a wink. It looked like he was breathing again. "Good job, P.T.," he whispered. "Details are important. They make a story pop."

"This is so cool," said Geoffrey, admiring the mess on the other side of the plate-glass windows. "They, like, totally trashed an entire room. That's way better than all that fake stuff blowing up at the Super Fun Castle."

Grandpa's smile grew wider.

"You and Gloria go take care of the Frolfers," he said. "I'll take over here."

We shot him a thumbs-up, and the master showman took the stage—the concrete patio in front of what used to be the Banana Cream Pie Room.

"Yes, ladies and gentlemen, that giant upstairs is quite famous. Used to have a goose that laid golden eggs. But he traded her in for one that made bacon."

Teed Off

Gloria hurried back to her souvenir shop; I corralled the panel of judges.

"That was fun!" I told them.

"Incredible special effects," said Ms. Matchy-Matchy. "Wonderfully realistic."

"That's why we call it the Wonderland. So, who's ready to meet the sixteen-year-old golf wiz they call Johnny Z?"

All the judges raised their hands.

"Well, he's right there, teeing off on the frog slide hole."

"How exciting," said Ms. Matchy-Matchy.

"Well, that's what the Wonderland is all about, ma'am: making dreams come true. For Johnny Zeng, it's hurling a disc at chain-link baskets. For others, it's having fun with friends and family in a place that feels like home. And for others, it's meeting Air Fur One, our resident disc-crazy dog!"

Right on cue, Air Fur One pranced over.

The judges oohed and aahed.

Air Fur One gave them a happy little bark.

More oohing and aahing.

That was replaced by the sound of grumbling and growling.

It wasn't the dog.

It was Bradley.

"Would you people *please* be quiet?" he shouted.

The judges gasped and took a step back.

"Yes," said Mr. Ortega, dropping into his best hushed-golf-announcer voice. "It's important for us all to stay as quiet as we can, for Johnny Zeng needs to step up to the plate and fling a home run."

"Manny?" said Bradley.

"Yes, Bradley?"

"Don't talk until *after* the toss."

"Right you are, Coach."

Air Fur One wagged his tail, sat down, and kept his eyes laser-locked on Johnny Zeng's Frisbee.

"Be the disc," coached Bradley.

"Be the disc," repeated Johnny Zeng, tightening his grip on the shiny black saucer. He bent his knees, going into a crouch, and flexed his disc-flicking wrist.

"He's going into his crouch," narrated Mr.

Ortega as quietly as he could. "Limbering up the all-important extensor carpi ulnaris muscle."

"Manny?" said Bradley. "Shhh!"

Mr. Ortega mimed locking his lips.

Finally, Johnny Zeng hurled his disc.

And of course Air Fur One took off after it.

"Air Fur One is going for the assist!" said Mr. Ortega, shifting into his excited play-by-play announcer voice. "Look at that dog go! A great individual effort!"

Six yards away from the frog slide, the dog leapt into the air, gave the camera an amazing barrel roll twist, hovered for half a second, and snared the shiny black Frisbee with his teeth.

He didn't dunk the disc into the basket.

He hit the ground and took off running!

Two seconds later, so did everybody else.

Come back here, you doggone disc snatcher!

Poor humans. They only have two legs to run on!

Doggy Paddling

Johnny Zeng leapt for Air Fur One just as the dog completed another lap around the pool.

He missed.

And ended up in the water.

"Help!" screamed the golf wiz, thrashing his arms. "I can't swim!"

Terrified, he was standing in the shallow end with his eyes closed, so I guessed he couldn't see that the water was only up to his waist.

"Hang on, Johnny," cried Mr. Ortega, dashing to the fence where we store our water-rescue stuff. "I'll throw you a life preserver!"

He did.

The Styrofoam ring on a rope bonked Johnny in the chest, because, like I said, he had his eyes shut. He was also flailing his arms a lot, and that makes it super hard to catch stuff.

Bradley stopped chasing after Air Fur One. The dog saw his chance and slipped down a path of pavers leading to the beach.

"Something like this would never happen at the Super Fun Castle!" Bradley told the world. "If a guest fell into one of our water features, trained professional lifeguards would immediately take them out of harm's way."

"He's not in harm's way," I said. "He's in the shallow end. It's the kiddie part of the pool."

"I can't swim!" blubbered Johnny.

"Rescue him," demanded the woman in the suit. No way was she jumping into the pool.

"Follow my voice up the steps!" shouted Gloria. "Marco!"

"Polo," said Johnny weakly. But he trudged through the water in the right direction.

Dill scampered over to help Gloria.

"Marco!" they both shouted.

"Polo."

"Open your eyes!" I yelled.

"Polo" was all the teen said in reply.

While Gloria and Dill kept Marco-Polo-ing Johnny Zeng out of the pool, I noticed that Bradley was grinning.

I marched right up to him before he could shout more nasty stuff about us to the judges.

"You wanted this to happen! You sabotaged us!"

"Of course I did, kid," he said with a sideways sneer. "Because that's how winners win."

A Well-Done Burger?

"**M**y pants are wet!" whined Johnny Zeng.

He had climbed up the three steps out of the shallow end of the pool.

"And the dog still has my disc!" growled Bradley.

"We have other discs you could borrow," I suggested.

"No!" said Bradley. "Only losers play with borrowed gear!"

"Agreed," said Johnny's agent. "Plus, we're looking at a product endorsement deal with a major disc manufacturer."

"Don't worry, you guys!" chirped Dill. "I know exactly how to make Air Fur One drop Johnny's disc!"

He ran over to the Banana Shack.

"Chef Jimbo? I need one burger—no bun, no

lettuce, no tomato, no onion. Just the meat—well done."

"Comin' right up."

Jimbo flipped a burger off the grill with his spatula and slid it onto a paper plate.

"Perfect!" said Dill.

He took off for the beach.

"Good idea, Dill!" I shouted as Gloria and I raced after him.

Down on the beach, I saw that surfer dude, Corky, helping a man with a very hairy back step into a kitesurfing harness.

But I didn't see Air Fur One.

All of a sudden, a clump of guys and girls in bathing suits hooted and squealed. Air Fur One was racing around their beach towels and coolers. He still had the shiny black plastic disc locked in his jaws.

"If that dog's teeth puncture the plastic, you're going to pay," roared Bradley, who'd raced down to the beach behind us.

Dill, who was amazing on the Frolf course, as you might recall, threw his circular meat patty sidearm. It went spinning through the air. Air Fur One dropped the disc and took off in hot pursuit of the burger, which arced slightly to the right—to where Corky was helping Mr. Hairy Back into his harness.

The dog barked, startling Corky. He dropped

a strap. A gust of wind blew in from the Gulf and filled the kite, which yanked Hairy Back off his feet and dragged him along on his belly like a sand plow just as Air Fur One caught the burger and started chowing down.

Welcome to Loserland

Corky chased after his customer, screaming. "I'm going to so totally sue you people! I went to law school!"

Then he shouted at the hairy guy being blown down the beach. "Bail out, brah! Don't ding the merchandise!"

Surprisingly, Bradley didn't run down to retrieve his precious, superspecial aerodynamic disc. Instead, he was studying Dill.

"You're that kid," he said.

"Excuse me, sir?" said Dill.

"The little whiner I tried to turn into a winner. You were the worst miniature golfer I've ever met."

"So?" I said. "He's awesome at disc golf."

"Enjoy your stay at the Wonderland, little man," scoffed Bradley. "It's where you belong."

Bradley headed back to the motel grounds.

"Don't you want your disc?" Gloria called after him.

"Nah. Keep it, kid. You can sell it in your rinky-dink souvenir shop up front. Call it a memento of the last professional disc golfer to ever set foot on your crummy little course."

Just when I didn't think I could feel any worse, Mr. Frumpkes charged up the beach.

"Aha!" he said, pointing at Air Fur One. "I see you're once again terrorizing the beach with your unleashed mutt. Well, guess what, Mr. Wilkie? I am, once again, calling the police."

He patted down his pockets, searching for his phone. Couldn't find it.

"Check that. I am going to my mother's house, where I will call the police."

"Do you need the number for 911?" I cracked.

"I know the . . . Oh, why do I even bother talking to children on my days off? That filthy beast is going back to the pound, where I imagine you found him."

"He's Jimbo's dog, not mine," I said as I rubbed Air Fur One's ears. "But I sort of wish he was."

"And did this Jimbo character rescue his dog from an animal shelter?" demanded Mr. Frumpkes.

"Yes."

"Well, why do you think that dog was in the pound in the first place?"

"Because—"

"That was a rhetorical question. I only asked it because I already know the answer. That nuisance was behind bars because someone knew they had a dud on their hands, so they dumped him. They knew it was a loser!"

Mr. Frumpkes stomped off to call the police.

And that was when it hit me: I had a choice to make.

A big choice.

And this time, I wasn't going to blow it.

Change of Heart = Change of Plans

Remember when I asked Dill to "take a dive" and lose his Frolf match against the judge's son so the Wonderland could win the St. Pete round of the competition?

Well, I sure do.

Because I shouldn't have done that. It sort of erased the whole *fun* part of the *Florida Fun in the Sun* contest.

Did I really want to be like funmeister Bradley, totally obsessed with winning, winning, winning—no matter what?

Nope.

I'd rather be like me and let the Wonderland be what it was supposed to be: wacky, goofy, silly, and, above all, fun.

And I had a feeling that if he had to make a choice, Grandpa would rather be remembered for all the smiles he had put on people's faces over the years and not for winning one magazine contest.

"Okay, guys," I said to Dill, Gloria, and Air Fur One, who was still looking up at me with an eager smile. "Huge change of plans."

"What?" said Gloria.

"It's time we all put on our pirate costumes and grabbed our squirt guns."

"Huh?" said Dill. "I'm supposed to put a pirate costume on top of my dog costume?"

"No. Forget being a mascot. Mascots are for super-professional places like the Fun Castle and Alligator Alley and major-league baseball teams. We need you in your pirate getup—the one you wore when we did that poolside raid to impress Geoffrey and his mom."

"Cool!"

"I'll grab Jack and Nate," I continued, basically making things up as I went along. "Gloria? Call anybody who isn't already here. Tell them to bike over here as fast as they can."

She nodded as she pulled out her phone. "I have our top cast and crew members on speed dial."

"Good. Because I want to do this thing in fifteen minutes."

"Woo-hoo!" said Dill.

Gloria raised her hand.

"Yes?" I said.

"What exactly are we going to do in our pirate costumes, precisely fifteen minutes from now?"

"What we do best: act like a bunch of goony goofballs and knuckleheaded maniacs. We're going to finish off this Frolf tournament with some Wonderland razzle-dazzle."

"Awesome!" said Dill.

Gloria was smiling. "I believe full-scale silliness will prove to be both actionable and deliverable."

Air Fur One barked. It sounded like he wanted in on the action, too.

We still had a lot of Frolfers enjoying the course. The judges hadn't left. They were getting a lecture from Bradley.

"This motel is a disgrace to the PDGA," I heard him say.

Johnny Zeng and his agent were long gone, but we still had an audience.

It was time to give them a show.

The Wackiest Place on Earth

We loaded up our squirt guns and water cannons and went to work.

"Pirates, ho!" screamed Dill, who ran out of his room in full pirate gear, waving his Tampa Bay Buccaneers banner.

Air Fur One leapt into the air to snag a Frisbee that just happened to be floating by.

"Hey!" a guy said with a laugh. "That pirate dog just plundered my disc, man!"

"Arrrrgh," I said in my best pirate voice. "That he did, matey. We be needing all your treasure. Do you know how much my piercings cost? A buck an ear."

My audience laughed.

"You know what they call a pirate who skips school? Captain Hooky."

More laughs.

"Arrrrgh, thank ye," I said. "I be here all week. But now we are going to attack ye. 'Why?' you might wonder. No real reason. We just arrrrrr!"

I fired the first shot in what would turn out to be the most incredibly ridiculous squirt gun, Super Soaker, and water-balloon battle ever waged in the state of Florida.

I aimed for Ms. Matchy-Matchy. She squealed and shivered. Fortunately, it was a happy squeal. Did I mention that it was ninety-eight degrees in the shade? I think she found my opening salvo very refreshing.

All the other pirates took that first squirt as their cue to start whaling away with their water weapons. The crowd loved it. Because being spritzed with cold water was a better way to beat the heat than chasing after flying Frisbees. Or maybe they loved it because it was exactly what the whole contest was supposed to be about: fun in the sun!

Even Mom and Grandpa grabbed water blasters and joined in. It was like an old-fashioned pie fight, but with water blasts instead of whipped cream.

Mr. Ortega's camera crew caught all the wacky action.

"Here you go, folks," said Gloria, handing out a bunch of water pistols to our guests. "No charge. It's today's free souvenir."

"How about towels?" giggled a Frolfer who'd just been soaked by Nate and Jack. "How much for a towel?"

"Those are free, too!" I shouted. "Because this is Walt Wilkie's Wonderland—the happiest place on earth!"

"Nope, nope, nope," said Grandpa, squirting Mom in the ear, which made her giggle like a little kid. "That's Disneyland. The Wonderland is the *wackiest* place on earth!"

Pirate Laugh Attack

In the middle of the mayhem, Mr. Ortega turned to his camera and said, "Isn't this what true sport is all about, folks? Playing games and having fun?"

"No!" shouted Bradley, who was blocking Gloria's prolonged water-cannon stream with a sideways disc.

Dill snuck up behind the big blowhard and lobbed a water balloon.

It was a direct butt shot.

It knocked Bradley off-balance. Arms whirling, he twirled, toppled forward, and belly flopped into the pool.

While Bradley was thrashing around in the deep end, a kid with what looked like his mom and dad strolled up to Mr. Ortega. The kid was twirling a Frisbee on his finger.

"Are you Mr. Ortega?" asked the mom.

"Yes."

"This is Johnny," said the mom. "Johnny Zeng. We're his parents. We're here for the interview?"

Mr. Ortega and I both blinked a lot.

"*You're* Johnny Zeng?" asked Mr. O.

"Yes," said the boy shyly.

"We received the message from your personal assistant Bradley late last night," said Johnny's dad. "About moving the interview back an hour?"

We looked at Bradley, treading water in the pool.

"Hey, hey, Tampa Bay," I said to Mr. Ortega. "You'd better get to it."

"Right you are, P.T."

Mr. O, his camera crew, the real Johnny Zeng, and his parents hurried off to find "better light."

I looked down at the fibbing funmeister.

"The first Johnny was a fake? You set the whole thing up."

Then it hit me.

"Of course! His 'agent' was Heather! That greeter girl from the Fun Castle on St. Pete Beach. Your fake Johnny works there, too. He's the guy from the parking lot!"

"You mean Todd?" said Bradley. "Prove it."

"Um, you just did," said Gloria.

"So?"

"So," said Ms. Matchy-Matchy, striding over to

join us poolside, "you and the Super Fun Castle in Tampa are hereby disqualified from this competition. Winners never cheat, young man, and cheaters never win!"

"What?" shouted Bradley from the middle of the pool, where he was being soaked by a twenty-one-water-gun salute. "That's stupid. Winners do whatever it takes to—*gurgle gurgle . . .*"

Nobody heard what other motivational words Bradley might've had to share.

Every time he opened his mouth, Dill blasted him with his squirt gun.

SSSLOOOSH!

Buh-bye, Bradley

Bradley finally climbed out of the pool and, with his pants all kinds of squishy, motorcycled away.

Meanwhile, Mr. Ortega landed his one-on-one first-ever exclusive interview with the *real* Johnny Z while the wackiness around the pool continued until sundown.

Later, after the judges left and the crowds drifted away, we were sitting around the Banana Shack—still laughing—when Mom's cell phone chirruped.

It was the folks from *Florida Fun in the Sun* magazine.

"Thank you for letting us know so quickly," said Mom after she'd heard what they had to say. "Oh, really? Good to hear. Thank you. We appreciate that. It's quite an honor and a surprise. Thank you again."

When she hung up, we were all, of course, staring at her. Well, everybody except Dill. He was busy munching on a pickle spear.

"So?" said Grandpa. "Did we win?"

Mom shook her head. "I'm afraid not, Dad. They said our production values weren't up to the same professional standards as those of our competitors."

Grandpa put his hand on mine. "Standards, schmandards. I thought you kids did a fantastic job, P.T."

"Thanks," I said. "Sorry if we let you down."

"Let me down?" he said. "No way. If folks had a few laughs, if we made them forget their work-a-day world for a few hours, well, fugheddaboudit, P.T. We won!"

I smiled. I'd guessed right. Grandpa was more interested in smiles than trophies.

"As we know," Mom continued, "the Super Fun Castle will not be moving on to the next round, either. Snarlin' Garland's Alligator Alley will be representing Tampa Bay in the state finals."

"Woo-hoo!" we all shouted, with Dill shouting it the loudest.

"But," said Mom, her grin growing, "the magazine and its partner, TripsterTipster dot com, want to award us a special prize. Apparently, our mystery shopper just raved about how much fun he had staying here."

"'He'?" I said. "So it was Jim Nasium, not Ms. Matchy-Matchy."

"Huh?"

"Sorry. That's just what we called our two primary suspects."

"Well," Mom continued, "like I said, we're being awarded a special prize."

"A trophy?" asked Grandpa eagerly.

Mom nodded. "And it's something Disney World has never won, because the magazine has never given the prize before. This is its first-ever Florida Kids' Choice Award."

"We did it, P.T.!" cried Grandpa. "We finally beat Disney! I knew we would. It was just a matter of time. Woo-hoo!"

He leapt up and did *his* happy dance. There was a lot of strutting, elbow flapping, and *bruck-bruck-bruck*ing involved.

When he was finished, Mom told us some more good news.

"They're putting a special article about us in the magazine. Plus, we're getting a five-star 'kids' top choice' rating on TripsterTipster dot com, and our trophy will be inscribed with a direct quote from our mystery shopper's review: 'In my opinion, it was the MOST fun I ever had!'"

"Yes!" said Dill. "Mom and Dad listened."

Huh?

We all turned to Dill, hoping he'd explain what *that* meant.

Once he finished nibbling his pickle spear, of course.

Not-So-Mysterious Shopper

"I was one of the mystery shoppers!" gushed Dill. "I couldn't tell you guys earlier because then it wouldn't've been a mystery."

"*What?*"

"See, my mom and dad run TripsterTipster dot com. That's why they've been so busy the last couple of weeks, crunching code in the room, helping out with the contest. Anyway, they convinced the guys at the magazine that if this contest was supposed to be all about fun family activities, they needed to hear from kids."

"So *you* were our mystery shopper?" I said.

"Correct," said Dill. "I was assigned to secretly review Captain Sharktooth's Pirate Cruise, the new Fun Castle, and the Wonderland Motel."

"Those first times we saw you," I said, "when

Mr. Frumpkes made you seasick and when Bradley was jumping ugly in your face, you were really doing research."

"Correct again. You made my vacation fun even when I wasn't a registered guest at the Wonderland. We were supposed to move to another motel, but, well, you guys have such excellent Wi-Fi and I was having so much fun doing stuff with you and Gloria that we decided to just hang here."

"I wonder why Ms. Matchy-Matchy and her son stayed here, then," said Gloria.

"Their air-conditioning busted," explained Dill. "They needed a place to stay over the weekend while it was repaired. Also, from what I hear, her son, Geoffrey, gets super bored super easy. You guys pulled off a major miracle keeping him happy for more than fifteen minutes. Guess it was a good thing we let him win that first Frolf tournament."

"I'm not so sure," I said. "I'm sorry I asked you to do that."

"Hey, even losing was fun, because you made me part of your team. And you know what, Mr. Wilkie?"

"What?" said Grandpa.

"If it were up to me, I would've given you the grand prize. Because this is definitely the funnest place on earth!"

Fun in the Sun

The next week, Gloria and I of course went back to school. It's the law.

Mr. Frumpkes called in sick the first day after the break. Guess he wasn't quite ready to talk to children again. Either that or he'd taken one too many cruises and made himself seasick.

Gloria and Grandpa's stock portfolio rebounded to its "pre-crash valuation," as she put it. The lawsuit against the edible-eraser company was thrown out. Apparently, the lawyer's daughter had faked the whole gagging incident.

"You have to trust your gut, P.T.," Gloria explained on the bus ride home. "You can't change with the winds, because the winds are constantly changing."

I nodded, because I thought I knew what she really meant. You win some; you lose some. What's really important is not just how you play the game but whether you enjoy playing it.

Jimbo promised us he'd bring Air Fur One to work with him on a regular basis.

"Have to keep him out of the kitchen, though, man," he told us over dinner at the Banana Shack. "Health code."

"We'll help you do that!" I said.

"Totally," added Gloria.

Mr. Ortega told us that both his Johnny Zeng interview and his squirt gun–battle audition piece, "The Joy of Sport," were too "soft" for the big dogs at ESPN. The job went to Biff Billington out of Philadelphia.

"Biff cleaned my clock," said Mr. Ortega. "But I will live to audition another day. Besides, the winters up in Connecticut can be cold. I prefer the warmth right here on St. Pete Beach."

He was looking at Mom when he said that. She was smiling. Then they both started blinking at each other.

Gloria and I almost barfed. My mom and her dad looked like they were maybe ten seconds away from making smoochy faces.

Later that week, Mr. Ortega ran his hysterical

"Wacky Water Beach Battle" feature on WTSP, and the very next day, he got a call from channel eight, WFLA—the NBC station serving Tampa and St. Pete.

They wanted to hire Mr. Ortega away from WTSP.

"And," Mr. Ortega reminded us, "NBC is the official network home of the Summer *and* Winter Olympic Games—all the way through 2032!"

Yep. Mr. Ortega had just found a sports dream even bigger than ESPN—the Olympics on NBC!

Grandpa and his contractor friend, Billy, completely repaired the Banana Cream Pie Room. I think this time they used Krazy Glue on the ceiling.

Also, Dad, if you're reading this, I want you to know that we still have our Frolf course set up around the property. It's not polished or slick, but it sure is fun.

So if you come to visit, bring your Frisbee.

And be ready to have a good time.

Because here at the Wonderland, that's what we do best.

We take care of each other. And we have a good time doing it.

Having a wonderful time!
Wish you were here!

P. T. Wilkie's
Outrageously
Ridiculous
and
Occasionally
Useful
Stuff

P.T.'s (Not Exactly) Patented Storytelling Tips

Some stories have more power than all the facts you can find on Google. Here are some of the tricks I use to give my stories SIZZLE!

"What if?": This question is where a lot of good stories get started. Daydreams, too. What if I dueled with a dolphin? What if I saved a family from an alligator? What if I lived in the coolest motel in the world? What if a world-famous game maker opened up a library? (Hey, someone should write a book about *that*!)

Hook: Give folks a dazzling, pie-in-the-face opening hook to get their attention; they'll want to find out what happens next! Grab them with the first sentence and never let go.

Planning: Every story has a plan. You have to sort of know where you're going before you start, or you'll never make it to the end.

Details: Details make a story sparkle! To really sell a tale, you need specifics. That's what makes fiction seem so real.

Skip the boring parts! Even though you need details, one of the best things about being a storyteller is that you don't have to put in *all* the details! Just pick the most interesting ones!

Conflict: When you're telling a story, you need conflict—or nothing is ever going to happen. No one wants to read about a nice kid who has a nice day and eats a nice snack with some nice friends. There has to be a conflict to resolve! A missing bologna sandwich can be a conflict! Or jewel thieves. Or an actor running away during a movie. Or a competition to be named the best family attraction on the beach! Create a conflict—then figure out an interesting way to resolve it!

Suspense: An exciting sense of uncertainty is an important part of any story. If the thread of your tale leaves your audience dangling, they won't dare let go. (Where *is* that bologna sandwich?!)

Twist: Sometimes you can see the ending coming from a mile away, so to keep things interesting, every story needs a beginning, a middle, and a *twist*. That might be why they call it "spinning" a tale.

A big finish: This is the most important part of any story. It's what people are really interested in: What happens in the end? Wow 'em with some razzle-dazzle!

Be sure to have fun!

P.T. and Gloria's
Fact or Fiction Quiz:
Fun-in-the-Sun Edition!

(Circle your answers and find out if you're correct at ChrisGrabenstein.com.)

1. The oldest surviving roadside attraction in the United States is a six-story elephant made of wood.

FACT or FICTION

2. Back in 1926, the success of a mini-golf course on top of a New York City skyscraper led to the opening of an additional 150 rooftop courses around Manhattan.

FACT or FICTION

3. Skee-Ball was originally called Box Ball because, in addition to rolling balls up the lane, players had to toss wooden boxes into the holes.

FACT or FICTION

4. Saltwater taffy's name comes from the process of boiling salt and sugar in salt water to make the treat.

FACT or FICTION

5. The famous Pacific Park in Santa Monica used to be so unpopular that the city council ordered its demolition.
FACT or FICTION

6. Dog lovers, rejoice! There's a twelve-foot-tall pug-shaped bed-and-breakfast in Idaho—potty trained and all!
FACT or FICTION

7. It would take a sloth an entire day to travel the distance of the world record for a flying disc throw.
FACT or FICTION

8. There are seven quintillion, five hundred quadrillion grains of sand on Earth.
FACT or FICTION

9. The world's oldest pleasure pier is Golden Gallop Pier on the French Riviera—it's supported by pillars made out of gold!
FACT or FICTION

10. A pier in Florida once held an inverted pyramid with live sea creatures inside!
FACT or FICTION

Acknowledgments

A big THANK-YOU (and a lifetime supply of sun-screen) to the crew that keeps the Wonderland racing along: Barbara Bakowski, eagle-eyed copy-editor; Linda Camacho, authenticity consultant and adviser; Shana Corey, editor extraordinaire; Nicole de las Heras, director de la art; Casey Moses, art designer; Polo Orozco, editorial assistant; Michelle Nagler, associate publishing and hospitality direc-tor; Eric Myers, extremely literate literary agent; and my wife, J.J., who lovingly makes me cut out the boring bits (I should write a book with her someday).

Ready for some PUZZLETASTIC fun from Chris Grabenstein?

Discover what James Patterson calls "the coolest library in the world," in the Mr. Lemoncello's Library series!

Nominated for 44 State Awards!

Turn the page to start reading Book One!

This is how Kyle Keeley got grounded for a week.

First he took a shortcut through his mother's favorite rosebush.

Yes, the thorns hurt, but having crashed through the brambles and trampled a few petunias, he had a five-second jump on his oldest brother, Mike.

Both Kyle and his big brother knew exactly where to find what they needed to win the game: inside the house!

Kyle had already found the pinecone to complete his "outdoors" round. And he was pretty sure Mike had snagged his "yellow flower." Hey, it was June. Dandelions were everywhere.

"Give it up, Kyle!" shouted Mike as the brothers dashed up the driveway. "You don't stand a chance."

Mike zoomed past Kyle and headed for the front door, wiping out Kyle's temporary lead.

Of course he did.

Seventeen-year-old Mike Keeley was a total jock, a high school superstar. Football, basketball, baseball. If it had a ball, Mike Keeley was good at it.

Kyle, who was twelve, wasn't the star of anything.

Kyle's other brother, Curtis, who was fifteen, was still trapped over in the neighbor's yard, dealing with their dog. Curtis was the smartest Keeley. But for *his* "outdoors" round, he had pulled the always unfortunate Your Neighbor's Dog's Toy card. Any "dog" card was basically the same as a Lose a Turn.

As for why the three Keeley brothers were running around their neighborhood on a Sunday afternoon like crazed lunatics, grabbing all sorts of wacky stuff, well, it was their mother's fault.

She was the one who had suggested, "If you boys are bored, play a board game!"

So Kyle had gone down into the basement and dug up one of his all-time favorites: Mr. Lemoncello's Indoor-Outdoor Scavenger Hunt. It had been a huge hit for Mr. Lemoncello, the master game maker. Kyle and his brothers had played it so much when they were younger, Mrs. Keeley wrote to Mr. Lemoncello's company for a refresher pack of clue cards. The new cards listed all sorts of different bizarro stuff you needed to find, like "an adult's droopy underpants," "one dirty dish," and "a rotten banana peel."

(At the end of the game, the losers had to put everything back exactly where the items had been found. It was an official rule, printed inside the top of the box, and made winning the game that much more important!)

While Curtis was stranded next door, trying to talk the neighbor's Doberman, Twinky, out of his favorite tug toy, Kyle and Mike were both searching for the same two items, because for the final round, all the players were given the same Riddle Card.

That day's riddle, even though it was a card Kyle had never seen before, had been extra easy.

FIND TWO COINS FROM 1982 THAT ADD UP TO THIRTY CENTS AND ONE OF THEM CANNOT BE A NICKEL.

Duh. The answer was a quarter and a nickel because the riddle said only *one* of them couldn't be a nickel.

So to win, Kyle had to find a 1982 quarter *and* a 1982 nickel.

Also easy.

Their dad kept an apple cider jug filled with loose change down in his basement workshop.

That's why Kyle and Mike were racing to get there first.

Mike bolted through the front door.

Kyle grinned.

He loved playing games against his big brothers. As the youngest, it was just about the only chance he ever got to beat them fair and square. Board games leveled the playing field. You needed a good roll of the dice, a lucky draw of the cards, and some smarts, but if things went your way and you gave it your all, anyone could win.

Especially today, since Mike had blown his lead by choosing the standard route down to the basement. He'd go through the front door, tear to the back of the house, bound down the steps, and then run to their dad's workshop.

Kyle, on the other hand, would take a shortcut.

He hopped over a couple of boxy shrubs and kicked open the low-to-the-ground casement window. He heard something crackle when his tennis shoe hit the windowpane, but he couldn't worry about it. He had to beat his big brother.

He crawled through the narrow opening, dropped to the floor, and scrabbled over to the workbench, where he found the jug, dumped out the coins, and started sifting through the sea of pennies, nickels, dimes, and quarters.

Score!

Kyle quickly uncovered a 1982 nickel. He tucked it into his shirt pocket and sent pennies, nickels, and dimes skidding across the floor as he concentrated on quarters. 2010. 2003. 1986.

"Come on, come on," he muttered.

The workshop door swung open.

"What the . . . ?" Mike was surprised to see that Kyle had beaten him to the coin jar.

Mike fell to his knees and started searching for his own

coins just as Kyle shouted, "Got it!" and plucked a 1982 quarter out of the pile.

"What about the nickel?" demanded Mike.

Kyle pulled it out of his shirt pocket.

"You went through the window?" said a voice from outside.

It was Curtis. Kneeling in the flower beds.

"Yeah," said Kyle.

"I was going to do that. The shortest distance between two points is a straight line."

"I can't believe you won!" moaned Mike, who wasn't used to losing *anything*.

"Well," said Kyle, standing up and strutting a little, "believe it, brother. Because now you two *losers* have to put all the junk back."

"I am *not* taking this back to Twinky!" said Curtis. He held up a very slimy, knotted rope.

"Oh, yes you are," said Kyle. "Because you *lost*. Oh sure, you *thought* about using the window. . . ."

"Um, Kyle?" mumbled Curtis. "You might want to shut up. . . ."

"What? C'mon, Curtis. Don't be such a sore loser. Just because I was the one who took the shortcut and kicked open the window and—"

"You did this, Kyle?"

A new face appeared in the window.

Their dad's.

"Heh, heh, heh," chuckled Mike behind Kyle.

"You broke the glass?" Their father sounded ticked off. "Well, guess who's going to pay to have this window replaced."

That's why Kyle Keeley had fifty cents deducted from his allowance for the rest of the year.

And got grounded for a week.

2

Halfway across town, Dr. Yanina Zinchenko, the world-famous librarian, was walking briskly through the cavernous building that was only days away from its gala grand opening.

Alexandriaville's new public library had been under construction for five years. All work had been done with the utmost secrecy under the tightest possible security. One crew did the exterior renovations on what had once been the small Ohio city's most magnificent building, the Gold Leaf Bank. Other crews—carpenters, masons, electricians, and plumbers—worked on the interior.

No single construction crew stayed on the job longer than six weeks.

No crew knew what any of the other crews had done (or would be doing).

And when all those crews were finished, several

super-secret covert crews (highly paid workers who would deny ever having been near the library, Alexandriaville, *or* the state of Ohio) stealthily applied the final touches.

Dr. Zinchenko had supervised the construction project for her employer—a very eccentric (some would say loony) billionaire. Only she knew all the marvels and wonders the incredible new library would hold (and hide) within its walls.

Dr. Zinchenko was a tall woman with blazing-red hair. She wore an expensive, custom-tailored business suit, jazzy high-heeled shoes, a Bluetooth earpiece, and glasses with thick red frames.

Heels clicking on the marble floor, fingers tapping on the glass of her very advanced tablet computer, Dr. Zinchenko strode past the control center's red door, under an arch, and into the breathtakingly large circular reading room beneath the library's three-story-tall rotunda.

The bank building, which provided the shell for the new library, had been built in 1931. With towering Corinthian columns, an arched entryway, lots of fancy trim, and a mammoth shimmering gold dome, the building looked like it belonged next door to the triumphant memorials in Washington, D.C.—not on this small Ohio town's quaint streets.

Dr. Zinchenko paused to stare up at the library's most stunning visual effect: the Wonder Dome. Ten wedge-shaped, high-definition video screens—as brilliant as those in Times Square—lined the underbelly of the dome like so many orange slices. Each screen could operate independently or as part of a spectacular whole. The Wonder Dome could become the constellations of the night sky; a flight through the clouds that made viewers below sense that the whole building had somehow lifted off the ground; or, in Dewey decimal mode, ten sections depicting vibrant and constantly changing images associated with each category in the library cataloging system.

"I have the final numbers for the fourth sector of the Wonder Dome in Dewey mode," Dr. Zinchenko said into her Bluetooth earpiece. "364 point 1092." She carefully over-enunciated each word to make certain the video artist knew what specific numbers should occasionally drift across the fourth wedge amid the swirling social-sciences montage featuring a floating judge's gavel, a tumbling teacher's apple, and a gentle snowfall of holiday icons. "The numbers, however, should not appear until eleven a.m. Sunday. Is that clear?"

"Yes, Dr. Zinchenko," replied the tinny voice in her ear.

Next Dr. Zinchenko studied the holographic statues projected into black crepe-lined recesses cut into the massive stone piers that supported the arched windows from which the Wonder Dome rose.

"Why are Shakespeare and Dickens still here? They're not on the list for opening night."

"Sorry," replied the library's director of holographic imagery, who was also on the conference call. "I'll fix it."

"Thank you."

Exiting the rotunda, the librarian entered the Children's Room.

It was dim, with only a few work lights glowing, but Dr. Zinchenko had memorized the layout of the miniature tables and was able to march, without bumping her shins, to the Story Corner for a final check on her recently installed geese.

The flock of six audio-animatronic goslings—fluffy robots with ping-pongish eyeballs (created for the new library by imagineers who used to work at Disney World)—stood perched atop an angled bookcase in the corner. Mother Goose, in her bonnet and granny glasses, was frozen in the center.

"This is librarian One," said Dr. Zinchenko, loud enough for the microphones hidden in the ceiling to pick up her voice. "Initiate story-time sequence."

The geese sprang to mechanical life.

"Nursery rhyme."

The geese honked out "Baa-Baa Black Sheep" in six-part harmony.

"Treasure Island?"

The birds yo-ho-ho'ed their way through "Fifteen Men on a Dead Man's Chest."

Dr. Zinchenko clapped her hands. The rollicking geese stopped singing and swaying.

"One more," she said. Squinting, she saw a book sitting on a nearby table. *"Walter the Farting Dog."*

The six geese spun around and farted, their tail feathers flipping up in sync with the noisy blasts.

"Excellent. End story time."

The geese slumped back into their sleep mode. Dr. Zinchenko made one more tick on her computer tablet. Her final punch list was growing shorter and shorter, which was a very good thing. The library's grand opening was set for Friday night. Dr. Z and her army of associates had only a few days left to smooth out any kinks in the library's complex operating system.

Suddenly, Dr. Zinchenko heard a low, rumbling growl.

Turning around, she was eyeball to icy-blue eyeball with a very rare white tiger.

Dr. Zinchenko sighed and touched her Bluetooth earpiece.

"Ms. G? This is Dr. Z. What is our white Bengal tiger doing in the children's department? . . . I see. Apparently, there was a slight misunderstanding. We do not want him permanently positioned near *The Jungle Book*. Check the call number. 599 point 757. . . . Right. He should be in Zoology. . . . Yes, please. Right away. Thank you, Ms. G."

And like a vanishing mirage, the tiger disappeared.

3

Of course, even though he was grounded, Kyle Keeley still had to go to school.

"Mike, Curtis, Kyle, time to wake up!" his mother called from down in the kitchen.

Kyle plopped his feet on the floor, rubbed his eyes, and sleepily looked around his room.

The computer handed down from his brother Curtis was sitting on the desk that used to belong to his other brother, Mike. The rug on the floor, with its Cincinnati Reds logo, had also been Mike's when *he* was twelve years old. The books lined up in his bookcase had been lined up on Mike's and Curtis's shelves, except for the ones Kyle got each year for Christmas from his grandmother. He still hadn't read last year's addition.

Kyle wasn't big on books.

Unless they were the instruction manual or hint guide to a video game. He had a Sony PlayStation set up in the family room. It wasn't the high-def, Blu-ray PS3. It was the one Santa had brought Mike maybe four years earlier. (Mike kept the brand-new Blu-ray model locked up in his bedroom.)

But still, clunker that it was, the four-year-old gaming console in the family room worked.

Except this week.

Well, it *worked,* but Kyle's dad had taken away his TV and computer privileges, so unless he just wanted to hear the hard drive hum, there was really no point in firing up the PlayStation until the next Sunday, when his sentence ended.

"When you're grounded in this house," his father had said, "you're *grounded.*"

If Kyle needed a computer for homework during this last week of school, he could use his mom's, the one in the kitchen.

His mom had no games on her computer.

Okay, she had Diner Dash, but that didn't really count.

Being grounded in the Keeley household meant you couldn't do anything except, as his dad put it, "think about what you did that caused you to be grounded."

Kyle knew what he had done: He'd broken a window.

But hey—I also beat my big brothers!

Astronauts made it to the moon. Can Piper make it through middle school?

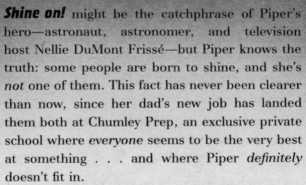

"Who do you want to be?" asks Mr. Van Deusen. "And not when you grow up. Right now."

Shine on! might be the catchphrase of Piper's hero—astronaut, astronomer, and television host Nellie DuMont Frissé—but Piper knows the truth: some people are born to shine, and she's *not* one of them. This fact has never been clearer than now, since her dad's new job has landed them both at Chumley Prep, an exclusive private school where *everyone* seems to be the very best at something . . . and where Piper *definitely* doesn't fit in.

When a mysterious alum launches a new award, the whole school goes into overachieving overdrive to win it. There's no way Piper can compete! Unless . . .

Is Piper finally ready to step out of the shadows? Can she stay true to herself and still find a way to shine?